Bridget

JULIA E. CAMMACK

Published by JULIA E. CAMMACK, 2024.

This is a work of fiction. Similarities to real people, places, or events are entirely coincidental.

BRIDGET

First edition. May 6, 2024.

ISBN: 979-8224339747

Written by JULIA E. CAMMACK.

Also by JULIA E. CAMMACK

Bella book 1 How One Woman Played the Game of Life
Bella Book 2 Winner Takes All
Bridget

Table of Contents

To all the amazing women who deserve to have books written about them and to my friends and family who put up with my idiosyncrasy and love me anyway.

Acknowledgement

I am indebted to Melissa Carroll who was kind enough to come every time I needed help formatting this book, to Adam Hays who listened and then created another amazing cover, and to my daughter Deanna who proofread the manuscript.

Prologue...

A calico cat lay sunning itself on a porch chair. If you knew nothing about cats, you would assume it was sleeping. Nothing could be further from the truth. The feline was aware of everything going on. She had witnessed the ball of yarn falling from the woman's lap and rolling across the floor. For a second, the cat wondered if it was worth her attention. It wasn't.

The dog paused long enough for her to acknowledge his presence with a pat and a lick. Over the years, dogs have come and gone. The cat was fond of this one. She had watched him grow from a pup. Now, his once black muzzle was sprinkled with white.

The children and grandchildren had been to visit, but now the sun was fading, Lucus would be coming to take the old lady in for supper. Ever since his father's passing, he had been her caregiver. Somedays, his stepmother thought he was Philip, and he hadn't the heart to tell her his father had been buried in the National Cemetery years ago.

The elderly woman was singing a lullaby in French. That was her language of choice today, but the cat liked it better when English with a southern draw was spoken.

The feline yawned and stretched. She, too, was getting old. She may leave tonight's hunting to the younger cats.

Table of Contents

Part One

Babies, Books, and Believing

Chapter 1

Too Many Questions.

The priest and the midwife were in the house with her mother. There was to be another baby. "A gift from God." according to the church. "If it was a gift, why did God keep sending them, then taking them back? Maybe He could send food instead." She had asked a nun this, and the only answer was a hard blow to the ear. She soon learned not to ask these things. That didn't mean she didn't think of them. All kinds of questions were running around in her head: "If the babies must be christened when they were born so that if they died, their souls would go to heaven, what about the babies born dead? Did they go to hell? That didn't seem right. What sins had they committed?" Asking for an answer to that question would have gotten her a whipping from Mother Superior.

Her brother and sisters were hungry and needed to be fed, but they had to wait until after the baby was born. The house consisted of one room, and that room was occupied. The little ones were beginning to cry. Her brother Patrick kicked the dirt and acted as if he didn't care if he ate. Earlier, she had gone to the fields to find Dandelion leaves. They could be eaten raw or cooked. The younger children didn't like them, but you ate what was available.

Her grandfather had shown her how to snare a rabbit. It could last for several days as a stew. She had been unable to leave the house, so now the larder was bare. Bridget had tried to show her brother how to catch one, but his coughing scared the rabbits off. There was blood in Patrick's snotty rag. That was not a good sign. Her beloved grandfather had died soon after he had begun to cough up blood.

The priest came from the house, followed by the midwife carrying a small bundle. The baby had been born dead. She couldn't say she was sorry about that. They couldn't feed the children they had. Both the priest and the midwife would want payments for their labor. The purse was as empty as the larder.

Chapter 2

The Stranger..

She lay in the tall grass, without moving, waiting for the rabbit to leave its hole, and thought about all kinds of things. So many questions still needed answers. She wondered about "It," the thing no one talked about. Bridget had seen dogs or cats mating and the rams mount the sheep. She knew how animals reproduced. During the year and a half, her father was in jail, there were no babies. Why not?

Why are some babies born alive and others dead? Some lived a short time, then some, like her brother, became ill after many years. Her baby sister, Rose, had lived to see her third birthday before becoming sick. Bridget had prayed so hard to the Virgin Mary to make Rose better. She promised all kinds of things. She would even become a nun if only Mother Mary would heal her sister. Rose died anyway.

A family in the village lived in a house with several rooms. They owned a pig and chickens, and most of the sheep belonged to them. The children didn't go to bed hungry or cry for milk. Why did some people have so much, and others suffer?

Deep in thought, she almost missed the rabbit that was peeking out, his nose twitching, seeking clues from the air.

Bridget forced herself to relax. He placed one foot out, then another, before deciding it was safe. She held her breath as the animal approached the snare. He was there. She pulled it tight. The rabbit struggled to get loose. Bridget quickly snapped his neck. There would be food for the table tonight.

As she rose with the bagged rabbit in her hand, flexing her muscles, cramped from being still for so long, Bridget realized she wasn't alone. A woman stood watching. A hood covered long white hair. Her clothing was ragged, and she walked with a staff. As many times as she had been in these woods, Bridget had never seen her. For a second, she was afraid, and then her curiosity took over.

"Who are you, and how did you come to be here?" she asked. The woman turned to go. "Wait. Don't leave. My name is Bridget." The woman disappeared into the trees. "How strange," she thought, but the rabbit must be skinned and dressed before being put in the pot, so Bridget headed home, still wondering what she had seen.

Chapter 3

A Gift.

Her brother grew worse as the days went by. Patrick tried to help but needed to lie down after laboring a little. The cough kept him awake at night, and he had no appetite. No one could explain why a healthy boy had suddenly become so ill. There didn't seem to be anything anyone could do. If prayers helped, he would have been cured yesterday. Bridget felt helpless.

Perhaps, if her father knew how ill his son was, he might return. After escaping from a British jail, he had been home for several days. People had warned him when the English had come looking, and he had slipped away into the night. Bridget didn't know where he was or if he knew there had been another baby. She knew he would be risking his life if he returned for even an hour, but she wished he could.

Bridget looked for the woman whenever she entered the woods to collect greens, a rabbit, or mushrooms. Sometimes, she felt as if someone was watching. There would be signs of her presence or a glimpse of her between the trees. Bridget began leaving gifts, a bouquet of lilies of the valley, a pretty bird feather, and a shiny rock, always in the same place. The next day, they would be gone. For some reason, Bridget knew it wasn't wise to ask anyone about the lady in the woods. Perhaps she liked having a secret that was all her own. It gave her something to think about besides her sick brother.

Bridget found a beautiful button. Usually, she would have kept it for herself, but today, she couldn't wait to share it with the stranger. She slipped away and hurried to her secret place. A package lay waiting there. Upon opening it, she found a small bottle containing a dark green liquid. There was a note written in a spidery scrawl. The problem was that she had never been taught to read. Leaving the button, she slipped the bottle and message into her pocket and hurried home.

The strange gift burned a hole in her pocket as she prepared supper for the children. Who in the village could she trust to read the note without asking questions? There was an old man who had been a teacher. He had become addled, and some said crazy. If he couldn't remember things, perhaps he could tell her what was written there and then forget. Bridget waited until the others were asleep, then made her way to his house.

The man opened the door. He asked her where she had been. Briget realized that he thought she was his child. That might make it easier for her to discover what was written in the note and keep it secret. There was a kettle on the fire. Briget made him a cup of tea and covered his knees with a blanket. After he was comfortable, she asked him to read the letter. He fussed at her, saying, "You could do this for yourself, daughter." but took the note and read it to her.

Bridget was astonished to discover that the message was instructions for using the tincture. The woman had sent it for her brother. How had she known Patrick was ill and needed medicine? Would it be safe to use? What if it was poison? Maybe the woman was a witch!

The man had dozed off. Bridget tucked the blanket around him and tiptoed out. Walking slowly home, she could think of nothing but what was in the note. There was a grave decision to make. If she chose to believe it would help her brother and she was wrong, he could die. If she didn't, Patrick would probably die anyway. What was the right thing to do?

When she arrived home, Patrick was coughing uncontrollably and having trouble breathing. Bridget needed to make a decision. She took a tiny sip of the tincture herself and waited. If it were poison, she would be the one to die. After several minutes, nothing happened, so Bridget gathered her courage and gave Patrick a spoonful of the liquid. It took a while, but his coughing slowed down.

She continued giving him the mixture throughout the night and into the next day. There wasn't much change in his condition, but he didn't seem any worse. Days later, when it looked as if they were running low, she carried the bottle back to the forest. There, on the stump, was a fresh bottle. "Thank you," Bridget shouted. She left the empty one and took the new one home.

Chapter 4

The Weight of Responsibilities.

Weeks had passed. Her brother still had a cough, and there was still blood, but nothing like before the strange woman had provided the magic elixir. For her, that was what it was. The church was taking the credit for his recovery. According to the priest, it was the prayers that had interceded. There was no reason to tell him anything different. It might even be dangerous. She had been slipping the liquid into Patrick's tea rather than openly giving it to him. He might ask questions about where she had obtained such a thing or what it was.

As Patrick improved, her mother grew worse. Ever since the baby's death, her mother would sit staring into space or weeping. She paid no attention to the children's crying. She wasn't interested in anything, including food. Bridget encouraged her to eat, but it was of no use. Her mother was wasting away before her eyes.

An adult would have been crushed by the weight of the responsibilities Bridget carried. She was still a child, but there was no one else to care for her siblings. He was doing better, and that helped, but Patrick was still not well. Then there was the question of money. It wasn't just the physical strain but the mental stress that was taking its toll.

Bridget worked hard to keep her problems to herself. She had taken up visiting the teacher who had deciphered the note. His family provided for him but lived in another village. She would make him a pot of tea and talk to him about everything, knowing he wouldn't remember any of it. He seemed to enjoy her company, and she felt a little better after unburdened herself. Sometimes, there would be food to take back for the children. They were both benefiting from this friendship.

Her mother had taken to wandering off. As the oldest, Patrick's job was to watch his mother. It wasn't possible to keep an eye on her all the time. Her brother had dozed off, and now their mother was gone. It was getting dark, and still, they hadn't found her. Some of the villagers joined in the search. It ended when her mother's body was pulled from the river.

Chapter 5

Liberated Tears.

Patrick was racked with guilt. No matter how often Bridget told him it was not his fault, he blamed himself for his mother's death. First, there was the question of whether she had wandered into the water or had drowned herself. If her death had been suicide, she could not be buried in hallowed ground. Thankfully, the priest decided that it was an accident. Their mother now lay in the church graveyard. The children were alone. No one knew if Bridget's father was still alive. If he did come back, the English police were waiting.

Her mother's sister arrived several days later. She was willing to take the younger children but had no place for Patrick or Bridget. Knowing the little ones had somewhere to go and would be cared for was a relief, but the older children would need to fend for themselves.

There were tears as the little ones were bundled off to their new family. Bridget knew it was the best thing for them, but that didn't make it any easier. There was a chance that she might never see them again. Bridget tried to keep a brave face for their sake, but her heart was breaking. She had lost her mother and now her sisters.

Bridget watched the cart until it disappeared. She fled to the woods as soon as it was out of sight. Once there, she collapsed, weeping. The tears flowed freely. She had kept them in, trying to be brave for the others, but now there was no stopping them.

A gentle hand on her shoulder caused her to look up. The lady was standing there. Bridget threw herself into the woman's arms and wept on her shoulder. How comforting it was to let go and grieve. She had been the rock for the others. At last, it was her turn.

Bridget had never seen the woman up close before. Her eyes were amazing. They changed color like a piece of rainbow glass. Her smile lit up her face, the way sunshine lights up a cloudy day. Bridget had assumed she was old, but now she realized that was not true. The woman's hair shone like the pearl necklace around the Madonna's neck in the church sanctuary. Ribbons of different colors were woven into her hair. Could this woman be a fairy queen, an angel, or perhaps something from the dark side? Should she be afraid? Was she in danger of being bewitched?

Chapter 6

Isadora.

When the woman spoke, it was in a raspy whisper. Bridget needed to listen closely to hear her. "My name is Isadora. I was once a healing woman in a small village. People came to me with their ills, and I did my best to help them. Most were grateful for what aid I could give. Many were healed, but some died. Not all things can be cured. They didn't understand that I was only a portal for Spirit's healing grace. It wasn't my place to decide who lived or died."

She rose and walked a few paces away. "I made tinctures and laid on hands, but it was always Spirit that healed. A woman's husband became ill and was brought to me. I have second sight and can look at people and see things. This man would not live so I made something to keep him comfortable on his journey. When he died, the woman accused me of killing him. She said I wanted him, and when he married her, I had poisoned him out of jealousy." Isadora sighed. "She accused me of being a witch."

"The people believed her. Everyone forgot the times their family or friends had been cured. They only remembered the ones who had died. A mob came to the house in the middle of the night. They tied my hands, put a rope around my neck, and dragged me down to the river. After fastening the end of the rope to a large rock, they threw me in. The weight pulled me down, and the rope tightened around my neck. I was unable to breathe. Fear engulfed me until I remembered that my life was in the hands of the Supreme Being, and I let go."

Bridget was spellbound, listening to Isadora's story. How could she have survived such a terrible ordeal? Isadora continued, " I stopped fighting the ropes around my wrists, and they loosened enough for me to remove a hand. The rock bounced off the river bottom and split in half. With the weight gone, I was able to surface and make my way to shore. I lay there, trying to catch my breath. All the while, the wet rope was cutting into my throat. At last, I was able to remove it, but my voice had been forever changed."

Bridget stared at her, "Then what did you do?"

"I gave thanks to Her for saving my life, and then I left that place and those who wished me harm and vowed never to heal people again. I stay hidden, away from everyone. The animals are all I need for company. They can be trusted. People can not."

Bridget could agree that most people were not trustworthy, but speaking of Her instead of God was earth-shattering. She couldn't believe anyone would say that. Bridget waited for Isadora to be struck down. When nothing happened, she said, "But you helped me. You gave me something for my brother. He would have died without your help. Thank you."

"You are right. I broke my vow. I couldn't stand by and watch you suffer. You don't know it yet, but you are a special person. The burdens you carried were threatening to break you. I couldn't let that happen. The future needs you, so I broke my vow. I took a dangerous chance. The chance you might tell of my existence. Now, you must decide what you will do without your family."

"My brother will go and live with the priest. I don't know yet what I shall do or how to continue giving Patrick your tincture."

Isadora nodded. " You must be careful. You, too, could be accused of witchcraft. The punishment is death. I see two paths for you. The choice must be yours." She rose and turned to leave. Bridget reached out to her. " What do you mean? Am I in danger? Isadora continued to move towards the trees and disappeared.

Chapter 7

A Good Idea..

Bridget sat in the teacher's parlor. She had made him a cup of tea and a poached egg. Sometimes, he forgot to eat, so she had taken up the task of making him food. He was lonely and enjoyed her company. Most of the time, he thought she was his dead wife or the daughter who lived several villages away. Once, he had wandered off, and it had taken hours to find him.

They talked about her mother's death and the loss of her siblings. He smiled and nodded his head without understanding. Bridget spoke of finding somewhere to live and some way to make money. She and her brother had dug potatoes for a few pennies, but now there were none left to harvest. No one in the village could afford to pay them, so she would need to go elsewhere to find work.

As Bridget was preparing to leave, an idea popped into her head. If Mac couldn't live with his daughter, how would the family feel about her caring for him? That could provide her with food, a place to live, and security for him.

The next day, Bridget spoke to the village priest. His recommendation could make a difference. Would the daughter consider having a caregiver for her father? Mac's daughter was overjoyed at the suggestion. Now, she could stop worrying. Bridget carried a few belongings to the teacher's house and settled in.

Bridget would rise early to start the fire and fix Mac's breakfast. If the weather were amiable, they would take a walk. She made sure to stop by the church and say hello to Patrick. While there, she always made him a cup of tea. He never realized there was a little extra in it.

After lunch, Mac would take a nap while Bridget tidied the house. She would prepare his afternoon tea, and then they would do lessons. The part of Mac that loved to teach was still present. He was happily teaching Bridget to read and write. That was an unexpected gift. The majority of people in the village were illiterate.

The two of them would sit talking until it was time for bed. Sometimes, what Mac said made sense, but he could stop mid-sentence, forgetting what he had been talking about. While Bridget felt safe telling him things, Isadora's story was not one of them. Bridget's everyday life wasn't a secret, but Isadora's presence was.

Chapter 8

To Seek Truth.

Because Bridget was afraid to leave Mac alone, her visits to the forest were few and far between. He was her responsibility now. If she wasn't there, he could wander off and be lost. Every few weeks, his daughter would visit, and it was then that she could slip off to the woods to seek Isadora.

If she found her, Bridget would ask Isadora all the questions that had been stored in her head for so long. Instead of punishing her for her curiosity, Isadora would do her best to answer. They would talk about everything, from sex to religion. How amazing it was to be able to speak openly about these things. Bridget's thought process was being stimulated, and she could feel her mind expanding. At last, she found the courage to ask Isadora about her use of the word "Her" when referring to God.

Isadora's idea of the Supreme Being, as she called God, was unlike anything Bridget could have imagined. Instead of a cruel, judgmental old man sitting on a throne, handing out punishments. Her God was like a parent, neither male nor female, a powerful force for good, someone kind and gentle. She could not explain why bad things happened to good people, including newborn babies and little children. One prayed for the higher good in all things and trusted in the results. People were not able to understand everything, nor should they. Isadora said she was not the healer but an intermediary who could call on God to fill the sick with healing light.

The church taught that one should strive to be perfect. The next thing they taught was that no one was perfect; everyone was a sinner. No matter how hard you tried, you would fail and be punished. Isadora claimed it was a way for the priests to frighten and control people.

Bridget didn't know what to make of this. Her whole life, she had felt guilty about questioning the lessons the nuns and the church taught. She had watched when these rules were broken by the very persons teaching them. Good people suffered, and bad people thrived.

Isadora told Bridget to decide for herself how she felt about these things. " Each of us must seek the truth that is right for us. When you find it, you will feel comfortable in your heart, but be careful. Do not speak of these things with anyone. There is a terrible punishment for a person considered a heretic. Even a child can be burned at the stake.

Bridget returned to the village more confused than ever. She trusted Isadora, but what if dark forces were at work here? Could the devil be trying to steal her soul? The Sunday sermon often discussed such things. That night, as she said her prayers, she asked forgiveness for her wicked thoughts and asked for the healing light to flow through her brother and make him well.

Chapter 9

A Goodby

Her lessons with Mac were becoming more complex. He would suddenly forget what they were doing. His mind wandered. Bridget needed to keep an eye on him even at night. He would wake after a few hours of sleep and think it was time to eat. The door must remain locked at all times and the key hidden, or he might leave. Mac would have fits of temper or begin crying. Sometimes, he would dress and insist that he was late and should be at the schoolhouse, teaching. It had been years since there had been a school in the village.

Bridget could now read simple things and write her name. The majority of Mac's books were thick and full of big words. She would sit and try to sound them out. Mac would help her pronounce them on a good day and explain their meaning, but those days were becoming fewer and farther apart.

Bridget had never given much thought to reading. She had no need for such a foolish thing. It wouldn't help her with her daily tasks or put food on the table. Now, she hungered for more and struggled to understand the words in Mac's books. Sometimes, he would read to her and answer questions about what some things meant. Her lessons with the nuns had been about rules and sins. The things Mac spoke about were of a world she never knew existed. Bridget had hated her classes, but now she waited eagerly every night, hoping Mac would be up to the task of sharing all that he knew. Her thirst for knowledge grew stronger as Mac's faded.

When the book was small enough, Bridget carried it to the woods when she visited. The one that she loved the most was about a faraway country. It had amazing pictures of mountains and beautiful waterfalls. How wonderful it would be to visit such a place! She couldn't wait to show the book to Isadora.

Isadora was becoming concerned. There had been increased activity in the woods, and while nothing had been said in the village, there was always the chance of discovery. It was time for her to move on, to find a new hiding place. Bridget, too, would be in danger if they were seen together. It was wonderful to have someone to talk with, but it would be foolhardy to put their lives in peril.

Bridget was struck dumb by the news of her friend's departure. She had come to rely on Isabella for council. The fact that she might be in danger because of Isadora's presence had been forgotten. Bridget had kept the secret of Isadora to herself. Surely, no harm would come to them.

Isadora had survived by trusting her instincts. It was time for her to leave. Before she bid Bridget goodbye, she gave her a blessing and a warning. "If you keep your own counsel and trust no one, not even Patrick, you may survive. Dark days are coming, so be prepared. Never stop believing in yourself. You will be faced with several different paths. Ask for guidance from your angels. Oh yes, you have angels that walk with you. Pay attention. Watch for the signs they will give you. You will have a long and amazing life if you stay true to your destiny."

Isadora kissed her on the forehead, turned, and soon disappeared into the trees, never to be seen again.

Chapter 10

Counting the Losses.

Bridget slowly walked back to the village. Isadora was gone. She had never bonded with another person before, not even Patrick. Her friendship with Isadora had grown over time. She felt as if a piece of her heart was missing. It had been a year of losses—first, her mother, then her sisters, and now Isadora. Patrick was talking about preparing for the priesthood, and she didn't know where her father was or if he was still alive.

Upon arriving at Mac's house, she encountered the village priest and Mac's distraught daughter. Her dear teacher had a heart attack and passed away while she was gone. The body was laid out in the parlor. A coffin was being prepared, and the three days of visitations would begin on the morrow. Family and friends would come by to pay their respects to Mac. She was to spend the nights watching over the body. Bridget wept not only for the loss of her teacher but for everything that had happened. The day that had begun with such promise had ended with terrible losses.

So many had known Mac, and he would be missed, but no one would miss him as much as Bridget. To make matters worse, Mac's daughter had informed her that they would sell the house and that her services were no longer required. Once again, she would be homeless. For over a year, Bridget had taken care of Mac. Her only compensation had been a place to live and food. Again, she would be out in the cold without a penny.

After all the visitors left, she would sit there with Mac's body. Instead of finding it scary, Bridget would discuss things with him as if he was still alive. It helped her think. There must be an answer to the situation. What could she do if there was no place for her in the village?

Isadora had told her that she had guardian angels watching over her. Where were they? When explaining this to Mac's corpse, she realized she had no idea where Isadora had lived. Bridget had never seen a dwelling of any kind, but there must be one. As a young child, she had been told tales of evil spirits and wild animals that lived in the deep woods, so she had never dared to go there. Tomorrow, while the family greeted visitors, she would search for Isadora's secret hiding place.

Over the next few days, she spent time in the woods whenever her help wasn't needed. Each day, she would go deeper and deeper into the forest. As skilled as Bridget was at reading the clues left by the animals, she almost missed it. She had passed a large outcropping of rock several times, and halfway up was a ledge with several bushes. As she turned to retrace her steps, something caught her eye. Isadora had told her to look for signs, and there it was on a bush, a blue hair ribbon fluttering in the breeze.

The bushes covered a narrow opening. Bridget bent down and squeezed through. She found herself in a large cave. Light filtered in from a small opening in the roof. Signs of someone having lived there were everywhere. In one corner, branches had been piled up and covered with moss to make a bed. A circle of rocks had held a fire. There was a stool, a small table, and a shelf with jars of herbs with strange markings, among other things. Bridget had found Isadora's hiding place.

Chapter 11

Finding Shelter

The day of Mac's funeral was cold and wet. It rained on and off all morning. By the time everyone arrived back at the house, they were all soaking wet. Bridget stirred the fire and put a kettle on to boil for tea. The men were passing around a jug of whiskey. Villagers had brought in food, and soon, everyone was eating, drinking, and telling tall tales about Mac.

After everyone had departed, Bridget cleaned up and put things away. It had been an exhausting few days. Before Mac's daughter left, she informed Bridget that she needed to take her things and be gone the next day before the furniture movers arrived. Bridget was too tired to care.

In the morning, she rose early, made a pot of tea, and had breakfast. Thinking about everything she had done for Mac, she felt he wouldn't mind if she helped herself to a few things, nothing that would be missed. There were several old coverlets and a shawl. She put a cup, a bowl, a spoon, two pairs of Mac's socks, his whittling knife, an old kettle, and a cracked teapot in a burlap sack. She added some tea, a potato, and an onion. Putting on Mac's cardigan and his old loden green cape, she took a last look around, then remembering her favorite picture book, she slipped it into her pocket along with another that had clever drawings of animals. Bridget bid farewell to the house that had been her home, and with a last look around, she turned and walked into the forest.

No one saw her leave or cared that she was gone. Mac's daughter wasn't familiar with everything in her father's house, so there would be no reason for her to accuse Bridget of stealing. Once settled, Bridget would go by the church to tell Patrick she was safe.

She returned to the cave and emptied her sack. Luckily, she had gathered firewood earlier, so it was dry. She soon had a fire going. In no time, the cave was warm. Bridget laid the covers on the bed, set the kettle on the fire, and made a cup of tea. There was an oil lamp but no oil. When she visited with Patrick, there might be some available. A large slab of wood lay by the entrance. With a lot of pushing and pulling, she could secure the cave. From the marks on the floor, it looked as if Isadora had done the same. Bridget was exhausted after the long day and ready for bed.

The light from the fire made strange shadows on the wall. Curled under the covers, Bridget's thoughts turned to the tales of wild beasts and demons. Remembering what Isadora had told her, she asked the angels to keep her safe. The next thing she knew, the morning light woke her.

The cave was amazingly comfortable. Bridget had seen Patrick and been given some lamp oil, a carving knife, and a cooking pot. She found that by going to the village at dusk, a hood covering her head and stooping over like an old woman, no one noticed. She no longer had something to put in Patrick's tea, which worried her. His cough sounded better, but it could return at any time. Every night, when she said her prayers, she asked that Patrick be filled with the healing light.

Chapter 12

A Rescue.

The forest floor had sprung to life with the spring rains. Greens were easy to gather, and the ferns were almost as high as Bridget's waist. Squirrels and rabbits were fat and plentiful, as were the fish. She had settled into her new life. A vixen had dropped a kit and then, after several weeks, disappeared. Perhaps she had been trapped or killed by a predator. Bridget rescued the starving little fox when she realized the mother would not be returning. All she had to feed him was broth from a stewed rabbit. He thrived on it and was now her constant companion. He slept with her and curled up on her lap while she read.

The title of the animal book was impossible to decipher. "Asophe's Fables" was difficult for her to pronounce, and the meaning of those two words was even harder to understand. The stories were relatively easy for her to read, and she loved the pencil drawings of the animals but missed Mac's explanations.

Bridget had placed a large basin out to catch the rain that entered through the roof in wet weather. She had climbed up the rock face to the small opening that let light into the cave. A natural protrusion protected it, so the water would not enter unless the rain came from a specific direction.

Weeks later, when walking through the forest collecting mushrooms for her supper, Bridget was suddenly aware of a lot of noise and activity. Leaving her basket behind, she crept forward until she could see what was happening. English soldiers had rounded up a group of men and boys and were marching them through the woods. Among them were Patrick and the priest. Patrick had a gash on his head, and the blood made it hard for him to see. A soldier was prodding him forward. A shot rang out. The soldier guarding Patrick was afraid that someone was trying to escape. He turned to help. Bridget reached out, pulled Patrick down into the tall ferns, and covered them both with Mac's green cape. She placed a hand over his mouth and asked her angels to protect them.

The military, having restored order, forced the group onwards. No one noticed there was one less prisoner. Bridget and Patrick lay there, hardly daring to breathe until they could no longer hear any noise. Cautiously, they raised their heads and looked about. The forest was unusually quiet. Like them, the world was holding its breath. Suddenly, a loud volley of shots rang out, and then the forest fell silent once more.

Patrick wanted to rush forward, needing to know what had happened, but Bridget forced him to accompany her back to the cave. Once there, she cleaned up his wound. Bridget asked him, "What had happened? Why were they there in the woods?"

Patrick explained that the British were aware of the Irish rebel's visits to their families. They had come to the village and demanded the men be turned over. When none came forward, they rounded up all the males, including the priest, and marched them out of the village.

Bridget's second question was about their father. "Had he been one of the men? Had he come back looking for his children?"

"There were no rebels in the village at the time. Some had been there earlier, but not our father. When the priest tried to stop the soldiers from entering the church, they pushed him aside. When I tried to interfere, I was struck. They ransacked the church, arrested us, and forced us into the woods." Patrick was feeling nauseous, and his head ached. He still wanted to check on his friends, but Bridget wouldn't let him leave. Between his wound and the fact that it was growing dark, it would be dangerous for him to take the chance. Whatever had happened, it would still be the same in the morning. Tonight, he must get some sleep.

Patrick wanted to argue with her, but he realized she was right. Stumbling around in the dark would be foolish, even without his head wound. He drank the tea she made for him, then lay down on a pallet on the floor and fell asleep. Bridget thanked her angels for keeping him safe.

Chapter 13

A Gruesome Discovery.

Patrick still had a headache in the morning but refused to stay. He must discover what had happened to the others. Realizing that he wouldn't wait, Bridget agreed to go with him.

They moved cautiously, making as little noise as possible, back to where Bridget had first seen Patrick and the soldiers. The tracks, left by so many, were easy to follow. They crept along the path, watching and listening for the enemy. The journey ended in a sunlit clearing. Bodies lay where they had fallen. Whether they were men, boys, or a priest made no difference. All of them had been killed. If Patrick had been with them, he, too, would be dead.

The two of them stood in stunned silence, staring at the bodies of their friends and neighbors. The English hated them, but to do this for no reason seemed unreal. Bridget began to shake and could not stop. Patrick lost his breakfast and then began to rage against the soldiers. He had talked about joining the priesthood, but the only thing he was willing to join now was those fighting for Ireland's freedom.

They must return to the village, gather everyone, and tell them what had happened in the forest. How would the women and children manage without the men? Life had been hard enough before this. How could anyone be buried without a priest? Would the soldiers still be there looking for the rebels? Would Patrick be in danger if he was found?

Patrick stood on the forest edge and watched as Bridget entered the village. People had been waiting anxiously for the men to return. Dreading this task, Bridget walked as far as the church and stood there. As the villagers gathered around her, she asked her angles for the strength to tell them of their loss. It had become natural for her to ask them for help and thank them for coming to her aid.

The look on Bridget's face told them everything. Before she could say a word, women began to weep and wail. Children didn't understand what had happened but knew something was terribly wrong. Bridget spoke of the bodies lying there in the clearing. Every male, including the priest, was dead. Some stood in stunned silence, and some beat their breasts and wailed louder. Bridget's heart ached for them all.

Chapter 14

Time to Go.

Patrick left to join the rebels. He hoped to find their father. Even if that didn't happen, he would be fighting the men who killed his friends and his priest. He was coming up on his fourteenth birthday and now would be considered a man and jailed or shot if caught.

Bridget realized people were now aware of her presence. No one had come looking for her, but she no longer felt safe. Some questioned how they found the bodies and why Patrick hadn't been shot with the others. Perhaps they thought they were spying for the enemy. Like Isadora, Bridget realized that it was time to leave. The question was, where should she go? Isadora's advice had helped so far. She would ask the Supreme Being and watch for signs.

Bridget stayed far away from the village, and when walking in her beloved wood, she took precautions. She listened closely for the sound of the military and others.

Bridget's fox had found himself a lady friend and was no longer interested in her. His trips to the cave were further and further apart. Soon, he would give up visiting her altogether. Bridget was no longer needed by her furry friend. This, too, was a sign that it was time to go.

She needed to decide what to take and what to leave. A coverlet and her other set of clothing were necessities. So were her books and Mac's whittling knife. At the last minute, she added the carving knife. Everything else would remain. Bridget had been happy in her cave home, but it was time to move on. She made a roll from her belongings, put on the cape, and stepped out into the sunshine. Bridget might not know where she was going, but she was on her way.

Chapter 15

Safety in Numbers.

Bridget wasn't alone in her wandering from town to town. People were looking for work everywhere. The church would give food to women and children when it was available, but there was little to go around. Sometimes, Bridget snared a rabbit or two and sold them in town. It was one way for her to make a little money, but few could afford to pay. Times were hard.

At first, she traveled alone, but Bridget soon found that was not the safest thing for a young girl to do. A man had offered her a warm place in his master's barn for the night. Tired from her long day's walk, she climbed into the hayloft, tucked her roll under her head, and fell asleep. She woke to find the man, with his britches down around his ankles, tugging at her skirts. Jumping up and seizing a pitchfork, she lunged at him. He staggered back, tripped on his pants, slipped, and fell from the loft.

He lay on the barn floor, screaming in pain, his arm twisted at a strange angle. Bridget seized her things, climbed down, and was out the rear door just as the farmer entered from the front. The noise had attracted his attention, and he came to find out what was taking place in his barn. Let the laborer explain his state of undress and how he had come to fall.

Realizing that there was safety in numbers. Bridget had joined a band of women and children. She had become used to being alone, but now the company of the little ones reminded her of her sisters.

After they stopped for the day, she would tell them stories about the animals from her book. They would sit enthralled as she recounted the adventures of foxes, rabbits, and others. It was the one bright spot in the day for both the children and Bridget. Their hunger forgotten for a little while.

Chapter 16

A Rebel Attack.

When the potato harvest was good, most were sent to England, with little left for the Irish. The crops had become diseased, and the potatoes rotted in the fields before they had matured. There were few to ship to Britain and even less for the people of Ireland. People had gone hungry before. Now, they were starving. Rabbits and squirrels became scarce as everyone searched for something to feed their families. Babies perished, and children grew thinner and thinner. There seemed to be no end to the misery.

There was a notice on a church door in Belfast. Bridget stepped up to read what it said. She understood enough of the words to see it was about leaving Ireland for work in the Americas.

For several years, you would be an indentured servant. After that, you would be free to go wherever you wished. It included a place to live and food. How bad could it be? Was there a chance to return if you didn't like it?

Bridget loved Ireland, but there was nothing for her here. Her brother was off fighting, but she had no way of knowing where. To leave and go to a new country would be a daring thing to do. Would she be any worse off there? She begged for a sign.

There was an attack on the Belfast police station. The rebels stormed the building, seized guns, and shot several police officers. Before the raid was over, the military arrived, overwhelmed, and killed many of the raiders. Those who remained alive were jailed. They would be tried, but the foregone conclusion was they would be found guilty and face a firing squad. Patrick had been among those arrested.

Bridget was considering what she could do to help. The men were heavily guarded and not allowed visitors. No one was able to bring them food or speak with them. If only she could send Patrick a note to let him know she was in Belfast and aware of what had happened. There would be a hearing in two days, and the expected outcome was grim.

She racked her brain, looking for an answer, but there was none. Bridget had been able to save her brother once, but now he was in terrible trouble, and there was nothing she could do about it. She felt utterly helpless.

Suddenly, the night was filled with the sounds of explosions. Armed militia had blown a hole in the jail wall to rescue their friends. The police were caught off guard, and some had been wounded or killed in the blast. The prisoners made a break for freedom, swarming through the opening. They were met with a hail of bullets from the arriving soldiers. Bridget ran towards the jail. She saw Patrick fall. She tried to reach him, but her way was blocked. The scene was one of complete chaos. Bodies lay everywhere. Police, rebels, and soldiers lay dead or dying.

The townspeople stood silently watching as the dead were separated into groups. Bridget saw them lift her brother's lifeless body and pile it on a cart with the other Irish fighters. People were afraid to admit that they knew the prisoners. They, too, could be charged as enemies of the British. The corpses were buried in potter's field without the services of a priest. Bridget had lost the last of her family. There was nothing left to keep her in Ireland.

Part Two

****

A New Path

Chapter 17

The Trip to a New Land.

Bridget lay on a hard pallet in the bowels of a ship. The smell was disgusting enough to make you throw up if you were not already nauseous from the pitch and roll of the waves. The odor of unwashed bodies, vomit, and other things hung in the air, making it hard to breathe. Too many people were crowded into the cramped space. Fleas and head lice had found happy homes. The biting and itching were almost enough to make you forget the smell. She had lost count of the days. How long did it take to get to a place named Baltimore?

She had signed a paper agreeing to work in return for room, board, and passage to America. No one had explained the accommodations she would share on the trip. It was too late to change her mind. She couldn't walk back to Ireland. A pot of fish stew with hardtack was sent down every night, but only a few were able to eat anything. The only clothing and books she began the journey with had been stolen. Bridget clung to the hope that things would improve once they reached land. It couldn't get much worse.

Land at last. The ship's gangplank was crowded with sailors unloading large boxes and other merchandise. The hatch was opened, and the people spilled out. Somedays, they had been allowed to venture up on deck for short periods to stretch their legs, but now, after so much time in the dark, they were like moles, blinded by the sunlight. The sailors laughed at the sight of humans staggering around as if drunk. Suddenly, a hose pumped cold seawater on the group to wash off weeks of filth and stench. The saltwater stung their bodies and burned their eyes. The deck became slippery, and several fell. Bridget, too, was having a hard time remaining upright. The deluge stopped as suddenly as it had begun.

The group was herded from the ship to a large warehouse. Bridget found walking on land difficult. After many days at sea, she had trouble adjusting to a floor that didn't roll under her feet. Back home, she had walked for miles without tiring, but after weeks of confinement, even the short walk was challenging.

Her clothing was drying fast due to the heat. The salt made them stiff, and it chaffed her arms. She couldn't imagine what anyone would think, seeing her as she was. Her hair hung in dirty twists, her dress was filthy, and she smelt horrid even after her dousing.

Once they were inside the building, a pompous little man called out names. As persons were identified, they were signed out and sent off. Finally, her name was called. A woman stepped forward. She told Bridget to follow her, then quickly left the building.

Bridget followed several paces behind the lady who gave her name as Mary. They walked briskly through the streets until they came to a two-story brick house with ivy-covered walls. Opening the side gate, Mary led her to the back garden. A large tin tub waiting by the pump was soon filled with water.

Stripping down to her undergarments, she stepped in and was quickly submerged up to her neck in the cold water. Mary took a pair of scissors, and her hair soon joined her dirty apparel. A large bar of soap and a razor were produced. Bridget scrubbed herself from head to toe, after which Mary shaved what hair was left, explaining it was the fastest way to ensure the head lice were gone. Everything would be burned. "Welcome to America!".

Bridget received clean undergarments and a dress that was a little big. She gathered it in at the waist with an apron. It would do for now. A dust cap would cover her head, and a bonnet should be worn when in public. Mary, too, had come to America as an indentured servant. Now, her time was coming to an end, and she must train Bridget to take her place.

Mary explained the family's background. It consisted of a doctor, his wife, and two children. As Quakers, their lifestyle would take a little getting used to, but they were kind and treated the help well, unlike some folks in town. "Best not to speak unless spoken to. You may have trouble understanding everything they say, and they will surely have trouble with your thick brogue. Try to rid yourself of it if you can. Many look down on the Irish. Come. I will show you through the house. The kitchen is where you will need to begin. You may want a bit to eat." Having said that, Mary turned and entered the back door. Bridget followed. Her choice to come to America might not have been so bad after all.

Chapter 18

The Job Description.

Mary was an excellent teacher. She taught Bridget all that was expected of her regarding the care of the house. They rose a little after four, lit the fire in the cook stove, and put water on to heat for the family. The jugs of hot water were carried up to the bedrooms and placed in washbasins. The pots were removed with the night's waste, emptied, rinsed, and returned to their place under the beds. Breakfast was made for the family, and while they ate, the covers were removed from the beds and put out to air.

After everyone had finished eating, there were dishes to clean. Depending on the day of the week, rugs would be beaten, floors scrubbed, and clothing washed and placed on the line to dry. There were always meals to prepare. While Mary and Bridget did the work in the kitchen, the mistress would join them to discuss what was to be served.

Mary explained that Abigail Taylor was the doctor's second wife, much younger than his first. She was a shy, mousie creature, much happier reading her Bible or sewing when she wasn't helping the doctor. While the children were relatively well-behaved, they liked to play pranks, and Abigail was intimidated by her stepchildren. It would take Mary's stern voice to calm them.

The children took to Bridget immediately. She thought about her sisters back home. They would be about the same age as these children. Caroline was six, and her brother Johnathan was almost five. Their mother had died giving birth to the boy. Mary had mothered them until Abigail had arrived. Abigail, who wasn't used to children, felt like the odd man out. The children sensed that. They were not always kind.

Where Abigail shone was in the office. Her bookkeeping was perfect. Every entry was neat and precise. Not a penny was out of place, and each one was accounted for. There, she was a different person. She could calm a weeping mother, prepare the doctor's instruments, and bandage an arm better than most. She was confident and sure of herself. At home, she felt like a fish out of water. Even at the Quaker meeting house, the socializing made her head hurt and her stomach tighten.

Doctor Daniel Taylor was a fine figure of a man, tall and slender with dark wavy hair beginning to grey at the temples. While he adored his young wife, he was oblivious to her troubles with domesticity. The house and children were just fine as far as he was concerned. When returning from visiting patients, the doctor would find a hot supper, happy children, and a neat home. That was all a man required. He didn't have any idea what it took to accomplish it or just how overwhelmed his young wife was.

Chapter 19

A Wedding.

The months passed quickly. There was always something to do. Mary taught Bridget everything she needed to know about housework and meal preparation. While she hadn't graduated to making cakes or pies yet, her loaves were proudly served at the supper table.

There were several gatherings at the meeting house during the week and all day on Sunday. Prayers were said before meals and bed, as well as for the sick or those considering sinning. Bridget wasn't always sure what sins people were considering or if the prayers ever stopped them from doing the sinning. She could see that robbery, injuring someone, and murder were grievous sins, but smiling at someone of the opposite sex or showing your ankle, along with other silly things, seemed too ridiculous to consider. Why would that be frowned upon by God?

Her hair was growing back and must be covered at all times so as not to tempt a man. No matter how warm the day, her dress must be buttoned to the neck and a white cloth neatly gathered there. Even in the rain or on a muddy road, one must be wary of lifting their skirt and exposing their ankles. Did people genuinely think these rules would keep someone from fantasizing about the opposite sex?

Mary's release from bondage was drawing near. Not only would she be free to go wherever she wished, but she had met a widowed baker who owned a small shop. They had declared their intentions to marry. Soon, she would be baking for their business instead of the Taylors. The children didn't want her to leave, but everyone else was delighted. Dr. Taylor would give the bride away. There would even be a small dowry. Bridget would miss her presence in the home, but she would be close enough to visit. They had become friends. Mary had been a bridge to the world she found herself in, helping her to navigate her new life.

The women's sewing circle had made a beautiful quilt as a wedding gift. Bridget had made her a nightdress with lace cuffs and delicate embroidery. A teapot with cream and sugar containers and six cups came from the family. Bridget hoped she would be as lucky when her time was up, and she, too, was free to leave. For now, it would be her job to keep everything running smoothly for the Taylors.

The wedding was a simple affair. The bride and groom left the meeting hall and went straight to the little shop on the high street. The home was on the second floor. A carriage house in the rear housed a bread van and a large cart horse. The bread was ready to be sold the day after the wedding. Quakers had no time for foolishness.

Chapter 20

Trouble Comes Calling.

Bridget managed the housework and the cooking, although it was a little more challenging than it had been with Mary's help. The children missed Mary at first but soon understood that Bridget, too, meant business when it came to their behavior. She expected them to do as she asked, but there was always a cookie or tart to sweeten their day. Time passed quickly, and she never had a reason to regret her decision to come to America. Bridget would always love Ireland, but life here was undoubtedly more comfortable.

Bridget had reached her fifteenth birthday. Mary had quietly wished her well, but there was no celebrating. Easter had come and gone without fanfare for the second time since her arrival. It seemed strange not to make a big thing of Easter or Christmas. Quakers did more praying and less celebrating. Bridget thought about Isadora's understanding of organized religions. Men, not God, made rules. The Society of Friends was kind but rather strict. She was smart enough to keep her thoughts about these things to herself and obey the rules.

With Mary happily ensconced in her own home, Bridget spent more time with her mistress. They discussed the weekly menu, the ordering of groceries, and the children. Bridget knew her place, but Abigail had found Mary intimidating and was more relaxed with Bridget. Perhaps the fact that Bridget was younger helped.

Dr. Taylor had finished his daily rounds and said goodbye to his last patient. Instead of visiting with his wife and children, as was his habit upon arriving home, he went straight upstairs to the bedroom. Bridget had heard him come in and prepared a cup of tea. When she didn't find him in the parlor, she went upstairs and knocked on the bedroom door. The door wasn't closed all the way and swung open. The doctor lay across the bed, gasping for breath. Bridget called out for Abigail and began loosening his cravat and unbuttoning his jacket. Abigail rushed into the room. Between the two of them, they managed to remove his coat and shoes. Several pillows under his head helped him to breathe a little easier.

Abigail explained that he had been having shortness of breath and chest pains for several weeks but had passed it off, relating it to the spring weather. He promised to seek a physician for a consultation when he had the time, but there was always so much to do.

The women took turns massaging his hands and feet. They heated rice bags to keep him warm when he seemed cold. They passed smelling salts under his nose and anything else they could think of to help. Bridget prayed for healing light to fill his body.

By the morning, he was able to sit up and take a little broth. His breathing was not so labored, and he was able to suggest things they could do to aid in his recovery. He assured them that he felt strong enough to get up. Unfortunately, the room spun when he tried, and he almost blacked out. The women quickly helped him back to the bed.

Bridget suggested that Abigail get some sleep. She would stay with the doctor. While she refused to leave the room, Abigail agreed to lie on the chaise lounge and rest.

Chapter 21

The Brother-in-Law.

The doctor was improving daily. He insisted that he was well enough to return to work. His caregivers were just as sure that he needed more time. Neighbors helped with the children and brought in food. Mary came to help with his care and allow the women to rest.

A physician had come to the house, and the diagnosis was that he had a serious heart condition and should take time to heal. Perhaps he should give up his practice altogether. Of course, Dr. Taylor would not hear of such a thing. That was the kind of advice he gave others, but it didn't pertain to him. He would be fine.

The women made him rest as long as possible, but he was determined to return to his practice. The doctor promised to limit his patient load, but the workdays became longer and longer as time passed. There were sick people who needed him. Weeks after he had returned to work, he was found slumped over his desk. There was no way to know when the attack had occurred, but he had been dead for several hours. Abigail was now a widow.

So many attended Dr. Daniel Taylor's funeral that the meeting house could not hold them all. The children he had delivered had grown into adulthood and were parents themselves. People owed their lives to the years of care he had given them. He had been a respected community leader and one of the Quaker elders. Abigail greeted them all personally, thanking them for coming.

Everyone expected her to go to pieces, but Abigail surprised them. She closed her husband's office, packed away all his books and papers, and boxed up the remaining drugs left in the clinic while running her household and caring for her children. His only relative, a brother, was also informed of his passing. Several weeks later, Steven arrived on Abigail's doorstep.

Abigail had never met her brother-in-law. Her husband hadn't told her much about him, except they had a falling out many years before. Bad behavior, including gambling and drinking, had caused a deep rift in their relationship, but as the brother and a male, he would now be in charge of everything.

When Abigail tried to object, she was told that he was right. The law was on his side. He would be the one to control the monies, the home, the children, and anything else that belonged to Dr. Taylor, including Abigail and Bridget.

Chapter 22

Walking on Eggs.

The household changed overnight. Stephen Taylor was not a man to be trifled with. The children were to be on their best behavior at all times. His word was law and could not be questioned by anyone, especially Abigail. Everyone felt as if they were walking on eggs.

Stephen ate alone in the dining room, served by Bridget and Abigail. The rest of the family ate at the kitchen table after he was finished. His fare was better than theirs. While they didn't go hungry, he always had the best of everything. Beer had always been part of the meal, but now there might be a glass or two of bootleg whiskey. Strong alcohol never had a place in their home before his arrival.

Some evenings, he would leave and not return until early morning. No one knew where he had gone, but upon arriving home, he smelt strongly of liquor and had difficulty navigating the stairs.

He would be in such a foul mood the next day that it was safer to stay out of his way, and Abigail found if she could slip a little laudanum in his beer, it helped. There was a ready supply in her husband's medical bag. Without it, Stephen was difficult to deal with.

The little boy had come into the house crying because he had fallen. He didn't stop when ordered to, and Stephen had struck him, saying, "Now you have something to cry about." Abigail loved her stepchildren. After that incident, she worked to keep them both away from him.

Bridget had noticed that Abigail was having difficulty keeping her food down. She tired much easier than usual. At first, Bridget assumed it was stress from the loss of her husband and the arrival of her brother-in-law, but it soon became evident that Abigail was with child.

She had never been able to conceive in the years when she and Daniel were married. How happy her husband would have been to know that there would be a baby. Keeping the pregnancy a secret from Stephen for as long as possible seemed like the wisest thing to do. Bridget took up the slack to allow Abigail to rest.

Stephen's behavior was becoming more and more erratic. He was still trying to put on the face of civility in public, but the drinking was getting worse. Many evenings, he passed out before even making it upstairs to his bed.

He was a nasty, mean drunk. Bridget had sported more than one black eye because she hadn't done something fast enough to suit him. She tried to be a buffer between him and Abigail, but one evening, while Bridget was helping with the children, he ordered Abigail to bring him another drink. When she told him there was no more, he cursed her and moved to strike her. Abigail dodged the blow, but in doing so, she tripped and fell. Stephen left her on the floor and went out to find more alcohol.

When Bridget found her, she was in pain. There was blood on her skirt. Bridget put her to bed with a pillow to raise her hips and give her something for the pain. Thinking of all Isadora had taught her, she did her best to direct God's healing light to her friend and the baby. She didn't know what else to do. The Quaker's belief that the light of the Supreme Being shone in every person was strangely comforting.

By the next morning, the bleeding had stopped, but Abigail would need to remain in bed for several days to ensure that all was well. How they would accomplish that with Stephen in the house was the question. Luckily, he didn't return until late that night and went straight upstairs to bed. The next few days were strangely peaceful. Perhaps the idea that he had pushed things too far had sobered him. Bridget counted her blessings, as did Abigail.

Chapter 23

Sharing the Truth.

The women tried to pretend everything was fine. They appeared at the meeting house as often as possible, but Abigail's public appearances had become limited now that her condition was becoming evident. Both children were in the Quaker school, learning to read and write. Bridget shared their lesson books, welcoming the opportunity to further her reading skills when she had the chance.

The Friends Society was not unaware of Stephen's behavior. For one thing, no matter how he tried, he always smelled of alcohol. The community did not condone strong drink. His meanness and cruelty escaped their notice. The women were careful to keep these things to themselves.

There had been a meeting of the church Elders, and they agreed to address the problem. They arrived one afternoon with the idea of speaking with Stephen about his drinking. He became enraged when he realized why they were there and ordered them out of the house. He accused the women of telling lies and trying to create trouble.

Bridget and Abigail did their best to stay out of his way. They sent the children to stay with Mary and her husband. A small amount of laudanum in his drink helped, but they never knew when he would fly off the handle and begin raging or breaking things.

To make matters even worse, a man had come to the house and accosted Stephen. There was a gambling debt that must be paid immediately. Stephen demanded that Abigail give him money. When she explained it was for groceries, he began breaking dishes, saying, " You don't need dishes if there is no food to put in them." She quickly handed him her purse. He paid the man, then left with the rest of the monies. When he returned later that night, he was very, very drunk.

The next day, Stephen slept till noon. When he finally woke, he felt so ill that he was unable to leave his bed. Stephen demanded food but failed to keep it down. He threw the plate across the room in a fit of pique. What he wanted was a drink, and as soon as he could, he left the house to find one.

Mary brought the children home and insisted the women tell her what was happening. Reluctantly, they explained Stephen's drinking, his cruelty, and his use of Abigail's money to pay gambling debts. In addition, he had threatened to sell the house and move to an unknown location. Their situation was becoming dire, but being completely alone would be worse.

Mary avoided coming to the house when Stephen was there, but the women knew they could call on her for help. If they were forced to move, who would be there to help when Abigail's baby was born? If Stephen was upset when the children made noise, what would he do when the baby cried? Mary could see the fear in Abigail's eyes. Such stress wasn't good for the mother or the unborn child.

The laudanum was almost gone. It was the one thing that seemed to calm Stephen down, but Abigail had no way to get more. Would Mary consider traveling to the next town to purchase some? It could be easily obtained as a sleeping draft or for pain. Abigail had hidden a little money and would pay for another bottle. If their life was hard now, what would it be without laudanum to temper his rage? Mary quickly agreed. She wished there was more that she could do, but what? Stephen, being male, was in complete control of the situation. Women had no say about anything.

Chapter 24

An Attack.

Stephen stayed drunk for a week. When he came home, it was to change his clothing and find something to sell. When she confronted him about taking a pair of silver candlesticks, Bridget was told to mind her own business, and if she told anyone, he would say she had stolen them. Bridget would go to jail, and Abigail and the children would be alone. Was that what she wanted?

Stephen stayed away as long as there was enough to pay for a drink. His absence sometimes lasted two or three days. The women were thankful for these times. They felt safer with him out of the house.

One night, after Bridget had gone to bed, Stephen appeared in her bedroom. He pawed at her nightdress. Frustrated, he ripped it. She tried to push him away, but he struck her, grabbed the pillow, and pressed it over her face. She couldn't breathe. Suddenly, he was on top of her. The pain as he forced himself upon her was terrible. She screamed and then passed out.

When she gained consciousness, Abigail was there bathing her and wiping away the blood. Bridget began to cry. Her whole body ached. Her torn clothing lay on the floor, and the bed was covered in blood. She was having difficulty speaking through her swollen mouth. Abigail insisted she make use of a medical bulb full of hot water and herbs to flush out her insides. If an indentured woman should become pregnant while still in service, she could have years added to her servitude.

Bridget began sleeping in the bed with Abigail, hoping that would protect her from another attack. Her monthly had appeared on time, but there was no one to stop him from raping her again. With each incident, there would be the threat of pregnancy.

Abigail was still sleeping when Bridget rose and went downstairs to start the kitchen fire. She bent down to place a log in the stove when Stephen appeared out of nowhere. He seized her from behind. Without thinking, she struck out with the piece of wood. It caught him on the shoulder. With a bellow of pain, he grabbed a knife from the table just as Abigail appeared in the doorway. She caught hold of his hand in an attempt to stop him. He pushed her hard, and once again, Abigail fell. The women screamed, and the children came running into the kitchen. When they saw their mother lying on the floor crying and in pain, they, too, began to cry. That was more than Stephan had bargained for. He grabbed his hat and coat and rushed out.

Bridget sent Caroline for Mary and the midwife. She helped Abigail to a daybed in the sitting room. It was too early, but the baby was coming. She put water on to boil and gathered towels. When Mary and the midwife arrived, she surrendered the children to neighbors and returned to do whatever was needed.

The baby boy entered the world silently. The midwife smacked him, laid him over her knee, and massaged his chest. She checked for mucus in his throat, and then, at last, he began to cry. It wasn't strong, but it was a welcome sound. They cleaned him with olive oil, wrapped him, and placed him in the open oven to keep him warm. Abigail had her baby. She named him Daniel, after her husband. If only Stephen stayed away, all would be well. The women waited in dread for his return.

Chapter 25

A Threat to the Baby.

Days passed without any sign of Stephen. No one knew where he had gone or when he would return. While people might speculate about what had happened in the Taylor household, no one knew for sure. Abigail and Bridget took turns caring for and standing guard over the new baby. If Stephen returned, what would his reaction be to the addition to his environment? What if the baby cried? There was no controlling an infant's crying or Stephen's rage.

Stephen was hungover and was in a filthy humor when he did return. Abigail took Daniel upstairs to nurse, hoping the baby would sleep after being fed. Stephen demanded Bridget prepare something for him to eat. He sat at the table drinking a beer, cursing at her for being slow. When he called for another beer, Bridget quickly gave him one, but not before adding a dose of laudanum. Stephen shouted for Abigail and insisted that she bring his nephew down.

With fear and trepidation, Abigail presented her child for his uncle's inspection. Stephen made snide remarks about how ugly and small the baby was, saying, "Just think how easy it would be to crush him like a bug." He pressed his palms together, imitating squashing something. Stephen laughed, delighting in the look of fear on Abigail's face. Once again, Bridget topped off his beer.

Abigail placed her son in the basket and set about helping Bridget prepare Stephen's meal. When he stood up and made an unsteady move toward the baby, Abigail quickly offered him another tankard, but not before adding laudanum. He sat back down and soon emptied it. Bridget placed the food before him, but he was having trouble holding his fork. His hand didn't work. Suddenly, he fell face down into the plate, slid from the chair, and lay on the floor. The women stood staring at Stephan as he struggled to breathe. They hadn't intended the doses of laudanum to cause him harm. All they wanted was to protect the baby.

Stephen had stopped breathing and just lay there on the floor. The baby began to cry, so Abigail picked him up and began to rock him. Bridget patted her on the back, picked up her shawl, and went to notify the authorities.

Because his brother had succumbed to a heart attack, no one questioned Stephen's death. He was buried in the cemetery next to Dr. Daniel Taylor.

Neither woman spoke of what had happened that evening or of the half-empty bottle of laudanum. All they had wanted was to stop him from hurting the baby, so each had added some to his drink. If Mary suspected anything, she kept it to herself.

Chapter 26

A Peaceful House

There was a strangeness between the women since Stephan's death. There was no way of knowing which of them had delivered the fatal dose or if it was the laudanum that killed him. Perhaps he really had died of a heart attack. The children had begun to relax, and the baby grew plump and happy.

Abigail was now in charge of the family finances. While a considerable amount of the money was missing, they could manage comfortably. Quakers live simply, so Stephen selling the silver pieces was of no great concern. The candlesticks had sentimental value because they had belonged to Abigail's family, and she had brought them with her when she married, but she gladly exchanged them for a stress-free home.

Bridget kept the house running smoothly and helped Abigail care for the children. Mary would visit often, and there was always something to be done for the Society of Friends. From time to time, there were grumbling and threats from the Puritans against the Quakers, but with Stephan gone, their lives were peaceful for the most part. Each day flowed into the next. The baby's giggle and smile were all they needed to brighten their day.

For Bridget, it seemed she had always been in America. Ireland seemed so long ago and so far away. It was hard to remember. Her servitude would soon be coming to an end. She could join Mary at the bakery or pursue employment as a nanny or housekeeper. There were choices to be made.

Would she remain in Baltimore? Stay where she knew people, or leave and travel to places she had dreamed of visiting as soon as she knew they existed? Bridget had worked hard to lose her accent, and now it was difficult to tell her apart from her neighbors.

Mary and Abigail asked her about marriage. There had been several young men at the Meeting House who had glanced subtly in her direction. After her experience with Stephens's vicious attack, the idea of being with a man was frightening. She avoided all contact with males. Many saw it as modesty, but the concept of intimacy filled her with dread. Many of the young women she knew were betrothed. They had families and dowries. She had neither. Those things weren't necessary if she had no wish to marry.

Chapter 27

A New Beginning.

Abigail's mother had written a letter asking her and the children to come home. Her parents were getting up in age and would welcome her company. Her father, Doctor Grant, was giving up his practice and retiring. The young doctor who would be taking his place could use someone with her skills to help in the office. The offer would include a small salary, and her mother would be happy to help with the children.

Other than Mary and Bridget, Abigail had no real friends in Baltimore. A change of scenery would be welcome, and her parents needed her. The house reminded her every day of Stephen's death. She had justified her part in his passing if she was the one to blame. The safety of her baby had been her top priority.

Since her husband's death, she had missed working in a doctor's office and helping with the patients. It didn't take her long to decide this would be in the family's best interest. Bridget would be leaving soon, and the big house would be hard for her to care for alone. The school in Washington was more advanced, and the children would have a better education. She would sell the house and put the gains aside for her son's college. Perhaps he would become a doctor like his father.

Abigail put the house up for sale. She gave several pieces of furniture to Mary and her husband for their new home. The old shop had been expanded, and part of the top floor was now used for storage. A small space could be converted into an apartment if Bridget chose to remain in Baltimore.

A cart was coming for the furniture Abigail wished to take. The rest she had sold. Bridget would accompany her on the journey to help with the three children. Bridget's bondage would be coming to an end in a few months, and she would be free to do as she pleased. Abigail would write a letter of recommendation in testimony as to her ethical character. Hopefully, Bridget would be able to acquire a position in either city.

The trip began early in the morning and was long but uneventful. The children were exhausted when the family arrived at their destination. The two women weren't in much better shape. All of them were having a hard time keeping their eyes open. Bed would be most welcome. Their heads had barely hit the pillow before they were asleep.

Upon waking, Bridget took a minute or two to remember where she was. The sunlight was streaming in the window. She had always been the first one up. It seemed odd not to be preparing for the family's breakfast. She dressed quickly, washed her face, and brushed her hair. Abigail and the children were already eating, and a place had been set for her. Bridget felt uncomfortable sitting at the same table as the family and being served by a maid. When she offered to help clear the plates and wash the dishes, she was told she was a welcome guest and should join the ladies in the drawing room for coffee. Bridget and Abigail had taken care of the house together, but Bridget always knew her place. It seemed rather strange to now be treated as an equal.

Chapter 28

The New Doctor.

Abigail's mother was a plump, friendly lady with bright blue eyes and a wonderful smile. Having her daughter and the children there made her happier than she had been in a long time. Her days were filled with cuddling the baby and playing with the children. Her husband was kind but had always devoted his life to his practice and patients. Even now, Doctor Grant spent most of his time with his replacement, bringing him up to date with everything necessary to make a smooth transition.

Abigail was helping the new doctor settle in. The fact that the man was handsome and personable didn't hurt. They were soon on a first-name basis. Those in the main house could hear their laughter from time to time. Her father's files were sadly muddled, and his handwriting hard to understand. She spent hours setting everything straight. The cabinets were filled with dusty boxes and bottles of pills. Not all were still viable. Putting everything in good shape would take days, not that Abigail minded. Spending time with her father's new associate, John helped to forget everything that had happened since her husband's death.

Abigail could see that her father was in no hurry to retire. The two doctors were busily making their rounds together. It was essential to make the clients comfortable with the upcoming changes. Her father had been their doctor for more years than most of them could remember.

Soon, the older children were enrolled in school, and a nanny was hired to come in five days a week to help with the baby. Abigail's mother loved caring for him, but it was too much for her to do alone. Bridget helped with the house, but her favorite place to be was in the library.

She dusted the books and arranged them on the shelves in order. Bridget had thought that Mac, her teacher in Ireland, had a remarkable collection of books, but here was a whole room devoted to every kind of literature imaginable. She was delighted to find "Aesop's Fables" among them. Her copy of the book had been a keepsake taken from Mac's house, but she had lost it during the ocean crossing. Her reading skills had improved significantly, but Bridget needed someone to explain the words she still couldn't understand.

Chapter 29

Time Passes.

Abigail had worn her widow's weed for more than a year, but now she and her mother had hired a seamstress to make her new dresses. There was a soft dark gray with black trim and a storm green with dark green trim. It was too soon for pastel or bright colors, but these were much better than the dull black. She wore a black skirt and a white blouse while working in the dispensary with John and helping with the patients.

Both she and John wore white cotton coverings over their clothing. The office had received a fresh coat of paint and new display cabinets. The latest medical implements lay under a towel, awaiting the next patient. It was the most up-to-date dispensary in Washington. More and more people required their services every day. Abigail was finding her life fulfilling once again and it was very apparent that she and John were becoming close friends.

Abigail's father had too much time on his hands now that he was seldom needed in the office. One day he chanced upon Bridget, trying to decipher some difficult words in an encyclopedia. Not only did he help her to understand their meaning and how to pronounce them, but he also suggested other books she might like. Soon, they could be found, heads together, discussing something she had read or a new idea she had discovered. Her thirst for knowledge was insatiable. His wife suggested that Bridget would make a fine governess or even a teacher with more training. It was time for her to think about her future now that her contract was coming to an end.

Chapter 30

A Future and a Fall

Bridget lay resting on the wicker sofa in the solarium. Her head hurt, her body ached, and her bruises were turning lovely shades of blue and yellow, but her mind was preoccupied. She thought back over the months following her release from indentured service.

Abigail's father had found her a sponsor, and she was busy studying. Soon, she would go before a board to be judged. If accepted, she would be a teacher.

Abigail's mother had suffered a stroke, and Bridget had stayed on to help with her care. John had asked for Abigail's hand in marriage, and as soon as it was proper, they would be wed. That fact was troubling to Bridget. The bruises on her body were nothing compared to the ache in her heart. How could she keep silent about what had caused her to fall?

Bridget had been in the library. The book she was interested in was on the highest shelf. She had climbed the ladder to access it and several more she might need. Bridget had been reaching for it when she felt John's hands reaching up under her skirt and tugging at her undergarment. In fear and hast, she turned, lost her grip, and fell.

John was gone when she came to, and others were trying to address her injuries. Her head hurt, and the room went round and round when she tried to sit up. At first, she couldn't remember what had happened, but then the terrible truth of why she had fallen came creeping back. John was not the honorable man he presented himself to be. How could she allow Abigail to marry someone who would do such a thing?

Bridget had considered the problem from all angles. When she confronted John, he denied everything. He had laughed and asked her who Abigail would believe, him or an ignorant Irish immigrant. She could go to Abigail's father, but there was no guarantee that he would believe her. She would lose the privilege of becoming a teacher, as well as the family's friendship. There was no way to prove what had taken place. She could only hope that John would slip up and get caught betraying Abigail before the wedding or that it was a one-time impulse and nothing like it would ever happen again.

Several weeks later, her worst fears came true. A maid who had been with the family for years accused John of trying to fondle her. Instead of being believed, she was charged with lying and was fired. Abigail was sure that the girl had made the advances. She told Bridget that women were always flirting with John, but he was above reproach.

Bridget wanted to warn Abigail about the fundamental nature of her husband-to-be. It was, however, obviously unwise to try. Abigail was convinced that her fiance had been maligned, and nothing could change her mind. Even the slightest suggestion that there could be a grain of truth in the girl's statement was met with anger.

Because a teacher must be of excellent moral character, any hint of impropriety on her part would spoil any chance she had of being certified or receiving an offer of employment. She had no choice in the matter. She must keep it to herself.

Chapter 31

Time to Move On.

The governing board had interviewed Bridget. Abigail's father's glowing recommendation as to her character made it easy to obtain her teaching certificate. Every week, a call for teachers appeared in the newspaper from as far away as California, so it should be easy to find a position.

Abigail and John had posted their bans in the church and were to be married in a few weeks. Bridget had been careful to avoid being alone with John. Listening to Abigail boast daily about how incredible her new husband was made Bridget ill.

As much as she would miss Doctor Grant, Abigail's mother, and the children, Bridget wished to be as far away from John as possible. She wouldn't be the one blamed if the marriage failed. Abigail was blinded by love. No one could enlighten her as to her husband's roving eyes and hands.

The country was growing at an amazing pace. Towns and cities were becoming increasingly civilized, with an insatiable demand for teachers. Churches ran many schools, but private and primary classrooms were springing up everywhere. Most people had only a fundamental knowledge of reading and arithmetic. Classes took place in one room, and children of all ages learned together.

The rich had a different idea unless you were female. Girls were taught basic literacy and arithmetic, as they were expected to keep the household budget solvent. Deportment and social graces were also in great demand. The boys had a much more complex curriculum. They must grow up to be businessmen or attend college and become lawyers, doctors, or even politicians. While the educational difference between males and females was noticeable, the gap between the rich and the poor was striking. The poor had little need for an education. The children were soon put to work in the fields or factories.

Bridget had written and sent several letters of introduction and copies of Doctor Grant's letter of recommendation to St. Louis, Cincinnati, and Charlotte. It would have been a good idea to teach a year or two in Washington before striking out on her own, but uppermost in her mind was the need to be far away from Abigail and John.

Chapter 32

A Visit With a Friend.

Bridget returned to Baltimore to visit Mary and her husband before leaving for her new position. A private school in Charlotte had offered her a monthly salary, and it included a small cottage. Bridget's only experience of having her own space was the cave that had sheltered her in Ireland. Now, she would have her own tiny home.

Mary was delighted to see her old friend. It had been more than a year since they had spoken. Letters had been exchanged, but it wasn't the same as being face-to-face. Soon, they were talking and laughing as if they had never been apart. Mary showed Bridget her lovely new home and the remodeled bakery containing the latest ovens and glass display cases. A fancy sign hung over the door, and a bell announced the clients when they entered.

The two women celebrated their good fortune. Mary was happily married with a thriving business and, a good husband. Bridget had earned a place in society as a teacher. Neither would have believed this could be their future when they came to America as indentured servants.

The night before her departure, Bridget confided in Mary, telling her of everything that had happened. She worried that somehow she had been at fault, the cause of the attacks. First, there was the man in the barn in Ireland, the rape by Abigail's brother-in-law, and now, the groping by Abigail's husband-to-be. Had she unknowingly sent the wrong message?

Mary had suspected that Stephen had raped Bridget, but the thought that Bridget would feel that somehow she was responsible for the terrible behavior of these men was a shock.

"You poor child. To my knowledge, you have never been anything but proper. There are kind and honorable men, and then there are the predators. You were vulnerable, and realizing you were defenseless, they moved in like the wild animals they were. Now, you will be on your guard against such men. As sad as it is, you were wise not to mention it to Abigail. The only person that would have been harmed would have been you."

Mary put her arms around Bridget and held her as she cried. Bridget had carried these terrible secrets deep inside for so long. It was a relief to be able to share these things with a trusted friend. She felt as if a huge weight had been lifted from her heart. That night, she slept soundly and woke to a beautiful sunlit morning, ready to begin her new life.

Part Three

****

Into the Future

Chapter 33

A Home and a New Position.

Bridget had been met at the dock by a smart little trap driven by a gentleman in livery. His teeth, when he smiled, were a fantastic contrast to the blackness of his skin. He placed her cases in the rear and helped her into the front seat. As they left the dock and reached the main road, he explained that the woman who owned the school had inherited money from her family and her husband. She had invested everything in the school. His pride in Mrs. Montgomery was evident.

Bridget had expected a schoolhouse. Her surprise was evident when they passed through ornate wrought iron gates and arrived at the most prominent house Bridget had ever seen. Thomas drove around to the back, and once there, he helped her down. A path led to a small cottage with a covered porch. He opened the French doors and safely deposited Bridget and her possessions inside.

" Madam is napping. She expects you to be at the big house at four. She will show you the school rooms and explain what is expected of you." he said, then, tipping his cap, returned to his rig. Bridget could hear him whistling as he drove away.

Bridget stood in the doorway, looking at the interior of the house. Everything was perfect for a single lady. There was a room with a couch and a rocking chair, a table and two chairs, and a display case. Beyond that, a bedroom with a bed, a chest of drawers, and an armoire for her dresses. The front veranda contained two wicker chairs and an end table. Stepping out the back door, she discovered a basin and a small stove. A set of dishes presented themselves in the cupboard. The exterior kitchen was well protected from the elements. There were pots of herbs by the back steps and roses bloomed by her front porch. Their scent filled the whole cottage.

Bridget filled a jug with water from the pump and washed away the journey's grim. The bed called to her, but she feared missing her meeting with Mrs. Montgomery, so instead, she removed her belongings from their suitcases and put them away in the drawers. Her books, including a copy of "Aesop's Fables," a gift from Dr. Grant, found a home in the glass case. The beautiful mantel clock that Mary had given her as a farewell gift sat in a place of honor. She stood back and admired her work. "All mine." she thought. "My first home."

As four o'clock approached, Bridget walked slowly up to the big house. She wondered which entrance she was expected to use when a young black woman in a maid's uniform met her in the driveway. She introduced herself as Joseph's daughter and instructed her to enter by the side door. Bridget was deposited in the drawing room to wait. Soon, Mrs. Montgomery joined her. How grateful Bridget was for her time with Abigail and her mother. Her manners were that of a young woman of means rather than an Irish immigrant.

Mrs. Montgomery was intimidating. She was tall for a woman and had a regal air about her. She never took no for an answer and assumed that everyone agreed with her. Bridget took a deep breath and introduced herself.

"I have read your letter and that of your mentor, Dr. Grant. Our girl's school is dedicated not only to the basics, but we intend to graduate educated women. I see no reason for women to be simpering idiots, reared only to please men. You do not appear to be such a creature. We will, of course, teach deportment and how to run a successful household, but our girls will be able to carry on an intelligent conversation. Since my husband's passing, I have made this school my life's work. It has an excellent reputation for graduating exceptional women. That is why I have chosen a female teacher this time rather than a man. What do you think about that?"

Bridget nodded her head in agreement. She followed Mrs. Montgomery from classroom to classroom. Some were obviously where sewing or knitting was taught, and one had a blackboard and bookcases full of books. Mrs. Montgomery explained that the whole bottom floor was dedicated to learning.

The kitchen was where the girls experienced meal preparation and planning. While there was a full-time cook, Mrs. Montgomery taught this class herself. She stated that her girls could prepare a lady's luncheon or an elaborate banquet with equal grace and knew the monies needed for each. While Bridget knew how to cook the basics, she hoped she would be allowed to attend these classes.

The music room contained a parlor grand piano. A teacher came once a week to give lessons to those who wished to learn how to play. The second floor belonged to Mrs. Montgomery.

A ballroom took up the entire third floor. A dance master was called upon once a month to demonstrate the art of the dance.

Several girls boarded at the school, and Bridget would be expected to escort them to church on Sunday. Her meals would be taken in the main house, while her kitchen would allow her to make tea, among other things. She would have a week to prepare the classrooms for her students and acquaint herself with the city. Thomas would be available to drive her wherever she wished to go. When school began, Mrs. Montgomery would meet with her weekly for an update on the student's progress.

All this was imparted as they passed from room to room. At the end of the tour, Mrs. Montgomery asked if she had any questions or requests. Bridget was so overwhelmed that she couldn't think of a thing. After thanking her benefactor for the chance she had been given, Bridget returned to the cottage to rest before supper.

Chapter 34

Living up to Expectations

The time had flown by, and they were halfway through the school year. Bridget had established a daily routine for the classes. She worked extremely hard to live up to Mrs. Montgomery's expectations. Her students were doing well. There were weekly meetings with Mrs. Montgomery to discuss their progress. From time to time, there had been suggestions made, but for the most part, her teaching had met with approval.

Next week, the gentleman overseeing all the district schools would arrive to test her students. Bridget was nervous but felt her girls were well prepared and would pass with flying colors.

Her little cottage was a constant delight. Vases of roses and other flowers from the garden filled the air with fragrance, and a bowl of fruit decorated the table. Bridget had purchased several more books, which now joined others in the glass case.

Thomas had two granddaughters who came nightly to her veranda to hear her read from "Asophe's Fables," or a book of fairy tales. They would sit there wide-eyed and spellbound as she told them stories. They made Bridget think about her sisters. They would be so grown up by now. Did they wonder about her? Did they even remember her? They had been so young the last time they had all been together. Were they married, and did they have children of their own?

The only thing that bothered her since her arrival in Charlotte was a disturbing incident that had happened several weeks before. Bridget had been visiting one of the small shops in town when a man began beating a young black woman in the street. He cursed her and threatened to kill her. Bridget was horrified.

Suddenly, a gentleman appeared from a nearby tavern. Catching the man's arm as he raised it to strike her again, he said," Hold on there. You don't want to damage this woman. She will be no good to you if she can't work. Whipping her will leave marks, making her difficult to sell. No one wants an insolent servant. I'm sure she has learned her lesson. Let me buy you a drink."

Bridget stared in disbelief as the two men returned to the tavern, and the girl picked herself up and hobbled away. She was so appalled at what she had just seen that she wanted to beat both men. Whenever she thought about what had happened, she would become angry once more. If Bridget ever met the person who had condoned such behavior again, she would certainly give him a piece of her mind.

Chapter 35

The Dance.

There was to be a cotillion to celebrate the end of the school year. The girls were too busy dreaming of the dance to do any work. Dressmakers were everywhere, sewing or making alterations. Bridget would be expected to chaperon her students, so she, too, had been fitted for a ballgown.

Staring at herself in the mirror, Bridget couldn't believe what she saw. An elegant stranger in the most beautiful mauve dress stared back. Mrs. Montgomery had helped her pick the fabric and now had loaned her amethyst drops for her ears and a delicate amethyst drop on a gold chain to wear. Bridget had arranged her hair in a gentle knot on her neck. Picking up her long gloves, she took one more peek at herself, took a deep breath, and slipped out the door. Approaching the big house, Bridget heard music. "This is going to be the most magical night of my life." she thought.

The ballroom was a blaze of light. The chandeliers reflecting in the mirrors threw back their images. A band played in one corner, and several maids passed among the guests with trays of canapes and drinks. Looking around at her young ladies, Bridget couldn't help smiling. She thought, my girls look like a bouquet of beautiful blooms in their colorful gowns. For some, this would be their last hurrah. Several would tour Europe now that they had graduated, and most would be engaged before the end of the year. To them, Bridget was an old maid.

Mrs. Montgomery stood by the balcony door, talking to a group of men. When she saw Bridget, she beckoned to her. Bridget became aware of the tall, dark man leading the conversation. He seemed familiar to her. Suddenly, she realized where she had seen him before. It was the gentleman who had condoned the beating of the slave. Anger rose in her throat. She quickly excused herself and retreated to the balcony.

Bridget stood there, breathing in the cool night air and trying to gain control of her emotions. This person was obviously a friend of Mrs. Montgomery and someone of importance. She must not make a scene. Suddenly, he appeared at her side.

"Have we met before, Mademoiselle?"

Bridget was trying not to scream at him. "We have never met, but I witnessed your horrid behavior when you condoned a man for beating his slave," she said. To make it worse, anger always made her cry. She stood there, glaring at him, the tears streaming down her face. Then he laughed at her. Without thinking, her reaction was to slap him.

He caught her hand in midair. "I saved that woman's life. He would have been twice as angry if I had publicly embarrassed him. She would have received an even worse beating when they were alone. This way, she had value. Hopefully, he will think twice before beating her again." He introduced himself, drew a handkerchief from his pocket, and handed it to her. " My name is Philip de Palmar, and you must be Bridget. Mrs. Montgomery spoke highly of your abilities as a teacher. You do, however, wear your heart on your sleeve. That may not be a good thing to do here in Charlotte."

Bridget accepted the handkerchief. "What do you mean by that?" she asked.

"There are those here who do not take kindly to what they call "Slave lovers." There is a great deal of grumbling about the "Yankees" wanting to free the slaves. The South is built on the backs of these people. Cotton is the money crop and could not exist without them."

Bridget considered his words. "Now, who sounds "anti-slavery"?"

Philip laughed. " Are you going to tell on me? I am just stating the truth."

Bridget said, "What about Joseph and his children? They seem content."

Philip explained that Mr. Montgomery had set them free before he died. It had been their choice to remain. They were a rare commodity. Freed negroes. Joseph's son had gone north, but the rest of the family stayed to help Mrs. Montgomery with the school.

Bridget remembered her duties. Instead of spending time with this fascinating man, she should be chaperoning the girls. Apologizing for misunderstanding his earlier actions, she excused herself and went to find her charges. Bridget was relieved to find there had been no problems while she had been otherwise occupied. She was the perfect guardian for the rest of the evening. If thoughts of Philip de Palmer wormed their way into her brain, they were quickly dismissed.

Days passed since their meeting. Bridget ached to ask Mrs. Montgomery about Philip. Who was he? Did he live in town? Was he married? She scolded herself for such curiosity. He was none of her business; she must put him out of her mind. Even if she had the answers to these questions, what good would that be? He was a man of some importance, and she was a school teacher from a humble beginning, but not thinking about him wasn't as easy as it should have been.

Chapter 36

Philip de Palmer.

Philip de Palmer was the middle son of a prominent planter. His older brother had been groomed to take over the plantation, and his younger brother was only interested in horses, women, and drink. Philip was the odd man out as far as his family was concerned. He had been sent to boarding school at six and spent most of the summers with his bachelor uncle in Boston. When it came time to choose a college, he decided to remain in the north. After graduation, he joined his uncle's firm.

The relationship with his father was strained, to say the least. As was typical for a well-bred southern lady, his mother never breastfed or cared for her children. They were paraded out for company, then sent off with the help. Out of sight, out of mind. The woman who had wet nursed him, kissed his scraped knee, wiped his tears, and tucked him in at night was a big, beautiful black woman called Mama Da. He had loved her with all his heart. When he was five, his father announced that he was too old to need a nurse, and Mama Da was sold. There had been no time to say goodbye. One day, she was there, and the next, she was gone. Even as a grown man, he couldn't find it in his heart to forgive his father for this or for the way he treated their mother.

When his father suffered a massive coronary and died while overseeing the whipping of a runaway slave, Philip saw no reason to contest his older brother's complete control of the plantation. His mother had remained there, but his sister-in-law was now the mistress of the house.

His mother was a fine example of how a southern woman was expected to behave, to be beautiful, charming, a delicate flower to be admired, a social butterfly. She lived up to this in spades. As the years rolled by, his mother became even more concerned with her looks. She had her maid pull her corset strings in tighter and tighter, trying to maintain her tiny waist. Every new cosmetic guaranteed to make her look younger appeared on her dressing table. She was delighted when someone commented that she couldn't possibly be the mother of grown men.

Philip felt a great deal of compassion for her. She was the prize his father had captured. As a young woman with many suitors, she had been the belle of the ball. Her social life had been filled with dances, flirtations, and expectations. The first years of marriage were exciting, but as time passed and the children came, her husband was happy to leave her at the plantation while he gathered with his friends or traveled to the horse races. He made no secret of there being other women in his life. Philip realized his mother had been lonely and depressed even before his father's death. Her dreams had failed to materialize, and now, she lived alone in an empty world. Lately, she had sought solace in liquor.

When his uncle, who had never married, died, he left the business and his money to Philip, who had used both wisely. Several large warehouses now bore the name of his company. In addition, there was a stout frigate that sailed from the Americas to England. Philip was in Charlotte to investigate the rumors that tracks might be laid to connect the coastal plains with Piedmont. What a boon that would be for Charlotte's economy. He was interested in purchasing shares in this railroad should it become a reality.

He had a home in Boston and a small townhouse for his mistress. He had also recently purchased a property in Charlotte.

Philip was never considered good-looking, unlike his father and brothers, but he was a great catch and never lacked female companionship. His siblings had inherited their mother's coloring and refined features and were extremely handsome. Philip, however, had a kind of animal magnetism that made women short of breath in his presence. Men, too, enjoyed his company and trusted him to have their backs in a fight.

Chapter 37

The Primary Guest.

Realizing how starved for companionship, his mother was at the plantation, Philip brought her to stay at his home in Charlotte for a few days. He arranged luncheons, afternoon teas, and dinner parties for her and her friends. His mother blossomed with all the attention, and he spent as much time as possible with her.

His older brother's wife arrived unexpectedly. While she was welcome to share in the festivities, he wanted his mother to be the primary guest. Unfortunately, his sister-in-law had a tendency to put herself forward whenever she could. He explained to Annabelle that this was his mother's time to be the queen bee, and no one should upstage her. Annabelle assured him that she would be on her best behavior. Philip hoped she would remember her promise.

The meeting of the North Carolina legislation to discuss the building of the railroad had kept him away for several days. Upon arriving home, he found his mother and Annabelle playing cards. An almost empty bottle of cordial and a glass sat on the table next to his mother. She was having trouble holding the cards, and when she tried to rise to greet him, she knocked over her glass. Philip caught her before she fell and helped her to the sofa. He rang for the maid, kissed his mother good night, and sent her upstairs to bed.

As soon as they were alone, he confronted Annabelle. She knew better than to encourage his mother's drinking. To drink because she was lonely and unhappy was one thing, but he was doing his best to keep his mother occupied and happy. He had emptied the liquor cabinet so there would be nothing to tempt her. "Where had the blackberry cordial come from?"

Annabelle admitted that she had brought it into the house. " A little drink after supper never hurt anyone. You are overreacting, darling," She smiled at him and placed her hand on his arm. Angrily, he pushed it aside.

"Not for you, but for someone like my mother who has a problem with alcohol, it will hurt her. You should know better. I can't be here to watch her all the time. You and my brother live with her on the plantation. Did you both not see that there was something wrong?"

"What do you know? You turn up and pass judgment on us. We are faced with caring for your mother day after day, week after week. You, a big wheel with money and no family responsibilities traveling from one exciting place to another, what do you know about how we live? How boring it is day after day, stuck out there in the middle of nowhere with no one to talk to. You arrive with all this fanfare, throw the whole place into an uproar, then depart again, leaving us to pick up the pieces." She burst into tears.

Philip gathered her into his arms. "Oh, Annabelle, I'm so sorry. I didn't take into consideration the fact that you are as big a victim as mother." She clung to him. How safe she felt in his arms. This was what she had dreamed of. This was where she belonged. Annabelle raised her tear-stained face and declared her intentions. She was his for the taking.

Philip was stunned. This was his brother's wife. What was she thinking? Sleep with his brother's wife? What kind of man would do such a thing? He gently extracted her from his arms and handed her a handkerchief. "I'm sure you don't mean that. You are tired and will feel differently in the morning."

Annabelle slapped him. "You think you are too good for us. Too high and mighty for us poor Southerners. Just because women swoon when you smile at them doesn't mean you can have anyone you want. Wait till I tell your brother how you made advances to me. He killed a man in a duel for my honor." She spun on her heels and ran out of the room. Philip watched her leave. A look of amazement on his face. Would she tell such a lie to his brother?

Chapter 38

Seeking a Companion.

After that night, while courteous, Philip took great pains never to be alone with Annabelle. On the other hand, she was polite in the presence of others but cold and very obviously angry. When his brother joined them for a night, Annabelle was affectionate and overly attentive to her spouse. Retiring with her husband at the end of the evening, Annabelle shot Philip a look of triumph. Philip stopped her as she passed by. "Think long and hard. If you insist on telling this lie, it will not be the first time you have accused someone. It may make people wonder why this keeps happening to you. My brother may also begin to wonder why. Do you want to take that risk? Even if he believed you, killing me would tarnish both his reputation and yours. I will not defend myself against him." he whispered. Annabelle glared at him and followed her husband up the stairs.

The next morning, Annabelle announced her intentions to return home with her husband. Philip's brother never remained away from the plantation for any length of time. There was too much that could go wrong.

Before his brother left, Philip asked what he thought about their mother staying in town. Caring for her had perhaps become a burden for Annabelle. On the other hand, his mother was enjoying the company of old friends. He had purchased a lady's maid, a cook, and a housekeeper to oversee the day-to-day running of the house. Arrangements could be made for a companion to stay with their mother in Charlotte when he was away. He would interview the young ladies and take care of the expenses. A solicitor could be hired to oversee everything. His brother considered it and agreed. After all, it wouldn't cost him a cent.

Philip had spoken with several young women about staying with his mother. Unfortunately, not one of them had met his expectations. She didn't need a nurse but someone to be a friend, a companion. He didn't want his mother to think she was being watched or judged because of her drinking. Instead, they should have fun together, play cards, visit friends, and do whatever his mother wished. He wanted her to feel as if this was her home and she was in charge. He would remain in Charlotte until he found just the right person.

Chapter 39

A Frightening Experience.

The coal-black pup Philip had brought back from Italy had grown into a huge, frightening beast with a heart of gold. People who knew the dog greeted him affectionately, while others crossed the road to avoid him. Beelzebub was Philip's constant companion.

It was such a beautiful day that Philip de Palmer had decided to walk to his bank. The dog was always up for a jaunt and trotted happily at his master's heel. As he rounded the corner, Philip was met by a strange sight. A woman stood in the middle of the road welding a buggy whip. Three men stood over a body. She was trying to drive them away, shouting at them to leave the man alone. Her whip had caught one of the men around the legs. He grabbed the whip and pulled hard, knocking her off her feet. She struggled to rise, and the men advanced towards her, laughing, but suddenly found themselves facing Philip and a large canine. The men stopped in their tracks.

"You don't have better things to do than frighten a woman? What kind of cowards are you? I suggest that you leave now or face the consequences." His tone was low and menacing. Sensing his master's anger, the dog curled his lip and let out a loud growl. One of the men stepped forward as if to challenge Philip, then changed his mind.

"N***** lovers. There is no place here for you. Come on. Let's leave them to it." The three men turned,

The woman was leaning over the body and trying to lift it to a sitting position. Philip went to help. Suddenly, he realized he knew them both. There was no time to ask what had happened. Bridget and Joseph could explain everything later.

Joseph groaned, then cried out in pain as Philip lifted him into the back of the buggy. He helped Bridget up, and she knelt beside Joseph with no regard for the dust and blood staining her dress. He drove as fast as he could to the Montgomery house with the dog running behind.

Philip carried Joseph into the front parlor and laid him on the couch. Bridget shouted for help. Mrs. Montgomery and Joseph's wife took one look and immediately set to work cleaning his wounds and bandaging his ribs. One arm hung at an odd angle. Philip wrenched it back in place. Joseph passed out from the pain.

One of the cuts wouldn't stop bleeding. Thread and a needle were produced, along with a bottle of bourbon. Mrs. Montgomery used her expertise to stitch the wound shut. When Bridget insisted that he be taken to the hospital to be checked out by a doctor, they looked at her in amazement. They explained that only white people could go to a hospital.

Bridget began shaking uncontrollably as shock set in. She had been brave while facing the danger, but now she couldn't stop trembling. Philip poured her a glass of brandy and insisted she drink it. Mrs. Montgomery fetched a warm coverlet and wrapped her in it. When the tremors had begun to subside, they asked her to tell them what had taken place before Philip arrived.

Bridget took a deep breath. " We were going to the shop to pick up fruit for supper. Suddenly, a trap raced by, almost tipping the carriage over. Joseph had brought down the whip on their horse to turn them away. Angered by his actions, the three men stopped and leaped down. They seized Joseph and pulled him from his seat, pummeling him with their fist. Once he was on the ground, they began kicking him. All the while, they were calling him terrible names. I grabbed the horsewhip and tried to drive them away. I was afraid they would kill him." She began to cry."I don't know what would have happened if you had not come by. I couldn't make them stop."

Without thinking, Philip put his arms around her. He held her tightly and let her cry. When she had calmed down, he gave her his handkerchief. Bridget was embarrassed. She had made a nasty wet stain on his jacket. He laughed, saying, " It goes well with the dust and blood I obtained while carrying Joseph."

Bridget's hair was loose and lay in tangles on her shoulders. Her eyes were swollen from crying, and her nose was red from blowing it. The dress that had been so pristine in the morning was now stained with blood and dirt. Philip wanted to hold her tight and protect her from the world and all its evils.

Chapter 40

The Answer to Problems.

Every day since the incident, Bridget asked that Joseph be filled with the healing white light. He would never again have the use of his right arm, but considering his age and the beating he had endured, he had made an amazing recovery. After days of discussion and consideration, it was decided that the best thing for him and his family was to leave Charlotte and join his son.

Joseph, his wife, their daughter, and grandchildren would take a boat north. Mrs. Montgomery would travel with them to ensure their safety. As much as Bridget would miss them, she understood this was the safest thing. If they stayed in Charlotte, they could be in danger. She had seen the hatred spewing forth from those men.

Bridget would never understand how one group of people could hate others so much that they wished them harm. Her thoughts returned to Ireland and all that had led to her brother's death. Because this was a new world, it did not mean that hatred wasn't alive and well.

There was a question about Bridget's place in the scheme of things. Going north with the others was an added expense, but it would not be proper or safe for a young lady to remain at the school by herself. Philip de Palmer had the answer to her dilemma and his own. Who better to stay with his mother than Bridget? She would be the perfect companion. She was charming, articulate, and trustworthy.

Bridget had put monies aside for living expenses while the school remained closed for the summer. Her little cottage was still hers to use as long as Mrs. Montgomery was in residence in the big house. Now, these plans had gone astray. The offer to attend Philips's mother came as a welcome surprise.

Once she met the charming elderly woman, there was no question of her refusing. She found Philip's mother delightful, and the feeling was shared by Mrs. de Palmer, who insisted Bridget call her Elizabeth or Lizzy. They were soon to be seen laughing over the antics of kittens or discussing the newest naughty book. The lessons she learned from Abigail and her mother and the school deportment classes were put to good use. Her manners were equal to those of Elizabeth's friends, and her charm and wit were soon welcomed at any gathering. Philip patted himself on the back. He could not have found a better confidant and friend for his mother. If he needed to be gone, he would have no trouble leaving her in Bridget's capable hands.

As to the possibility of a threat from the three men who had accosted Bridget and Joseph on the road, his dog would deter any problems Bridget might face from them. Beelzebub was now as content to remain at Bridget's side as Philip's. The dog would protect the house and the women in his absence.

Chapter 41

Bridget in Charge

An urgent letter had come from Philip's home office. He must return immediately. Such a trip might take several weeks, so he took Bridget to meet his solicitors, Messrs. Jordan and Jordan. Any problem that arose while he was gone was to be reported to them immediately. Philip had given explicit instructions on what actions must be taken in all instances. They would have complete jurisdiction over his mother's care and the property in Charlotte when Philip wasn't available.

After the horrific experience with Abigail's drunken brother-in-law, Bridget understood the need for legal protection from family. Philip was making sure that his mother and his property were protected. The moment Bridget felt anything was amiss, she was to send for the solicitor. Bridget was not to worry about it being a false alarm. Philip explained that while he loved his brothers, he didn't trust them. It was better to be safe than sorry.

His mother was unhappy with his leaving, but he promised her a lovely party when he returned. She and Bridget should spend their time while he was away, preparing a list of guests, deciding what would be served, and choosing the entertainment. He suggested they should have the dressmaker create new ballgowns for them both. This would be the event of the year. Anyone who was anyone would be begging to attend. It gave his mother something to look forward to.

Before he left, Philip spoke to Bridget in private. "Please understand my concern. I do not wish to say anything detrimental about my sister-in-law, but I am afraid she is somewhat domineering. You are responsible for my mother. It is crucial that Annabelle not be allowed to take charge. She doesn't believe that my mother has a problem with drink. I trust you. Remember, you speak as my authority. If she tries to run roughshod over you, refer her to the Jordan law office."

Bridget had met Annabelle only once. Annabelle had been so solicitous and sweet that Bridget was on her guard immediately. There was an air of insincerity as she gushed over Philip's mother and praised his choice of Bridget as a companion for Elizabeth. Annabelle had obviously been upset. Why had he chosen Bridget and not her? The final insult was to find that her mother-in-law had given Bridget permission to call her by her first name and, worse, by her pet name, "Lizzy." Bridget needed no warning about Annabelle. She had met her kind before.

Chapter 42

Preparing for a Party.

Bridget used everything she had learned since coming to America to keep Philips's household running smoothly. His mother was a delight. Bridget had taught her new card games, and she was teaching Bridget how to crochet. Mrs. de Palmer napped after lunch. Bridget took this time to write to Mary and also to Abigail.

The letters to Mary were returned with regularity. Unfortunately, the correspondence with Abigail was not. Mary's letters were full of good news. She had become the mother of a little boy, a big surprise at her age. Both she and her husband were over the moon at such a blessing. With the help of Elizabeth, Bridget was trying to crochet a blanket for the new arrival. While it wasn't perfect, it was made with love.

As Philip had predicted, Annabelle had paid them a visit, but while Bridget had been polite and welcomed her graciously, there was never any doubt as to who was in charge. Bridget thanked her for any advice she offered, served her a delightful afternoon tea, and then, with a smile, waved goodbye as her carriage drove away. Annabelle left with no illusions. Her rage was uncontrollable. Her one thought was how to bring this woman down. Annabelle couldn't decide which one she hated the most, Philip or Bridget.

Bridget argued that she had a lovely dress worn only once for the dance at the Montgomery house. It seemed extravagant to order another. Philip insisted that both she and his mother were to have the newest fashions available in Charlotte. Fabrics had been purchased from as far away as New York. Elizabeth had selected a grey brocade with silver lace. Bridget had been torn between a moss green and a primrose yellow satin. The dressmaker had been a frequent visitor to the house for design selections and fittings. Hairdressers were commissioned for the big day.

The house was cleaned from top to bottom. Chandeliers and mirrors were polished to within an inch of their lives. Extra servants had been hired for the evening. Philip was due home in a day or two, and everything must be ready. Bedrooms had been prepared at the Montgomery house for out-of-town guests, and Annabelle, her husband, and his younger brother would stay in Philip's guest rooms. Bridget had never met Philip's brothers, but Elizabeth would have all three sons with her for the first time in a long time. Bridget wasn't sure if the upcoming party or the presence of her sons made Lizzy the happiest.

Chapter 43

Pleasure and Pain.

The party had been an enormous success. No one wanted to leave. The musicians gave up at four in the morning and put their instruments away, but the guests lingered. The sun came up in time to light their way home. All agreed that it had been the best party ever.

Elizabeth was exhausted and had gone to bed around midnight. Annabelle's husband had also gone to bed, but Annabelle and Philip's younger brother had danced the night away, flirting outrageously. Bridget, too, had a wonderful time. She stayed at Philip's mother's side until Lizzy left the party, then she was free to enjoy the festivities. She had danced with several gentlemen, including Philip's younger brother, Nathaniel. The best dance was with Philip. The music seemed to have a special magic, and she wished that dance would never end.

Bridget rose late the following morning. When she arrived in the dining room, she found everyone had eaten. Annabelle had ordered breakfast in her room, and the three brothers had gone to look at a stallion to be auctioned off the next day. Lizzy was still basking in the glow of the party's success. Thank you notes had been pouring in all morning.

Most of the night's revelry had disappeared, and the house was almost restored to normal. There was still silverware to be polished and put away, tablecloths to wash, and beds to be stripped. Elizabeth was too tired to help and lay down for her nap early, so Bridget took care of everything that needed to be done.

Annabelle came downstairs, asked Bridget to bring her a cup of coffee, and settled herself on a chaise. Wishing to be polite, Bridget poured them both a cup, sat down, and asked if she had enjoyed the party. Annabelle smiled sweetly. "I always have an enjoyable time when I am with Philip. He is an amazing man and an incredible lover, don't you think?"

Bridget gasped and nearly dropped the cup she was holding. What was Annabelle saying? Annabelle and Philip were lovers? How could that be? Annabelle was married to Philip's brother. Philip was honorable and a gentleman, or was he? Was he just another man who could not be trusted?

Annabelle realized she had accomplished everything she wanted to. The pain she had inflicted on Bridget was visible. She would enjoy twisting the knife and watching this woman suffer. People must find out it didn't pay to cross Annabelle de Palmer. She would have her revenge on Philip as well.

Chapter 44

Mistrust and an Attack

Days had passed since the party, but Annabelle's words had been etched into Bridget's heart and brain. She felt ill every time she recalled Annabelle's casual remark. She had been unaware of her intense feelings for Philip and how much she had trusted him. How could she have been so wrong? How she missed talking to Mary. Some things can't be discussed in a letter. Bridget wanted to flee to her little cottage, bolt the door, and never leave.

Lizzy had not improved with rest. Instead, she was becoming weaker with each passing day. Special dishes were made to tempt her but rejected after a few bites. Philip had brought in specialists to treat his mother, but they could find nothing wrong. As much as Bridget wished to leave, Elizabeth needed her. She sat by the bedside or massaged Lizzy's feet, all the while envisioning the healing white light flooding the frail body of her friend. How quickly things change. A month ago, they had both been well and happy.

Philip remained unaware of Bridget's feelings. Instead, he attributed her curt replies to stress about his mother's illness. In addition, his younger brother, Nathaniel, had become a constant visitor. Philip was beginning to suspect the visits were as much to see Bridget as their mother. He hoped he was wrong.

Nathaniel made Bridget uncomfortable. He reminded her of Abigail's husband, John. He was always complimenting her appearance or the care she gave his mother. Nathaniel stood too close, and his hands lingered too long any time there was an opportunity to touch her. It wasn't anything she could put her finger on, but she worked to keep space between them.

Bridget had been in the dressing room, fetching a wrap for Elizabeth. Nathaniel assumed that no one was present but his mother, who was napping. The maid brought Lizzy a hot chocolate, placed the tray on the bedside table, and turned to go. Nathaniel grabbed her around the waist and ran his hand up under her skirt. The girl whimpered in fright. Stepping into the room and seeing this, Bridget was transported back in time. She remembered the assaults she had endured and let out a loud curse.

Philip let the girl go, and she ran from the room. Bridget stepped towards him, shaking with anger. "How could you? She is still a child. Just because she is a servant doesn't mean you can do whatever you wish with her."

"A servant? She is a slave, and I can do whatever I wish. She would have been broken in long ago at my father's plantation. Who are you to tell me what I can and can't do? You are the servant. A servant with airs far beyond your station. Pretending to be so pure and innocent. Annabella and I have a bet on whether or not I could seduce you, but I have grown tired of playing that game. I am finished being a gentleman." Nathaniel seized Bridget's wrist. She raised the other hand to fend him off.

Philip had been working in his office. Suddenly, Beelzebub rose, growling. The hackles on his back were in full array. Philip opened the door, and Beelzebub was down the hall in a flash with Philip on his heels. The dog hit the door full-on, and it burst open just as Nathaniel grabbed Bridget's other wrist. She kicked him as hard as she could, and he lost his balance. The next thing he knew, the dog stood over him, snarling.

Philip stood in the doorway, trying to make sense of the scene. "What the hell is going on?"

Nathaniel tried to sit up, but Beelzebub growled louder and showed his teeth. "Get this devil off of me. He should be destroyed. He is dangerous."

Philip called the dog to his side and ordered him to sit. "I will ask again, what is going on?"

Bridget stamped her foot. "He and Annabelle have a bet. He was to seduce me. When that didn't work, he attacked me. If he tries that again, I swear, I will kill him." As Nathaniel scrambled to his feet, she kicked him again. Seeing the look on his brother's face, Nathaniel sought refuge behind a chair.

Philip kept his clenched fists at his sides, not daring to move. He was afraid of what he would do. Trying hard to keep himself under control, he demanded that Nathaniel tell him everything.

Nathaniel blamed Annabelle. It was her idea for him to seduce Bridget. "She knew you were fond of Bridget, so she wanted to spoil it for you. If she couldn't have you for herself, she would poison it for you both. Annabelle told Bridget that you were her lover."

"So when your charms didn't work, you forced yourself on Bridget. What kind of a man would do that? I am ashamed to call you brother. I shan't kill you, but I will give you the thrashing you deserve." Philip tore the chair from Nathaniel's grasp and sent it crashing. His first blow drew blood, and he lifted his fist to strike again. A cry from the bed stopped him in mid-air. His mother was trying to get up. The only words she uttered before falling back on the bed were, "Please don't hurt him."

Chapter 45

The Burden of Guilt

The doctors said that Elizabeth had suffered a stroke. As a result, she was paralyzed on the left side, and her speech was slurred. Whether or not there could be any improvement was doubtful. Philip carried the burden of guilt for this. It might not have happened if he and his brother hadn't been fighting, but Nathaniel's actions had been atrocious. It was hard to believe that Nathaniel could behave so obnoxiously towards any woman, but to attack Bridget was unimaginable. Philip's anger had been tempered by his mother's stroke, but it still burned bright within him. Annabelle and Nathaniel were as responsible for his mother's condition as he was, but he would deal with that later.

Nathaniel had returned to the plantation. He was no longer welcome in Philip's home. Their older brother had come to check on his mother, but his wife Annabelle remained home. She had pleaded a sick headache. Philip was thankful for that. He wasn't sure he could have kept a civil tongue in her presence. Moreover, he was convinced that neither Annabelle nor Philip had told his brother what had proceeded the stoke.

A woman had been hired to care for Elizabeth. She had worked with stroke patients before with extraordinary results.

Bridget tried to ease Philip's guilt. The doctor had said his mother's stroke could have happened at any time, and perhaps she had experienced tiny ones before. That would explain her failing health.

Lizzy didn't seem to be in any pain and had forgotten the fight that had proceeded the attack. Friends came to visit, and while she couldn't speak, she could write notes with her right hand. Elizabeth's appetite improved, and Bridget happily prepared her favorite foods. The highlight of his mother's day was when Philip would read to her.

Mrs. Montgomery had returned home, and the school year would soon begin. It was time for Bridget to go back to her cottage. She remembered how she had longed to do so when she had believed Annabelle's lies. She was torn between returning to teaching or remaining with Elizabeth.

It had become a daily pleasure to share a smile with Philip or listen to him read to his mother. Once again, she trusted him and delighted in his company. Then there was her companion and hero, Beelzebub, the recipient of many a treat. The problem was that she couldn't find a plausible excuse for staying. Elizabeth was in good hands, and Mrs. Montgomery needed her.

Chapter 46

Revealing a Secret

Bridget had tidied up her cottage, put everything away, and was settling in. The school year was off to a good start, but she still had time for visits with Elizabeth.

The night before she left for her home, she and Philip had an intimate talk. He wished to make his intentions clear. Philip had agreed that it was prudent for her to return to her cottage and the school. Nothing must compromise her reputation. He did tell her that she would be missed, not only by his mother, but he, too, would miss her. If she had no objections, he would make arrangements with Mrs. Montgomery to call on her in the big house as it would be improper to visit her at the cottage.

He explained that he had been in a relationship with a woman up north for several years but had ended it since meeting Bridget. There was something else they needed to discuss, but that could wait for another time. He wanted there to be complete honesty and trust between them. He admired Bridget's lack of guile, purity, and innocence and wished to pursue their relationship. How could she tell him she wasn't the innocent woman he admired? Bridget was torn between happiness at the thought he was interested in her and the fear of revealing her past. How could she tell him about the rape?

Mary had told her it wasn't her fault, but how would Philip react?

Mrs. Montgomery was happy to act as a chaperon for Bridget and Philip. She liked and admired them both and felt that they were well-suited. Some might think that Bridget was not Philip's social equal. It wasn't anyone else's business if it wasn't important to him. Mrs. Montgomery wondered if it bothered Bridget because it was evident that something was not right. At the first opportunity, she sat Bridget down and questioned her.

Bridget hesitated. The only person with whom she had shared the secret of that terrible night had been her friend Mary. While she liked and admired Mrs. Montgomery, she wasn't sure what her reaction would be. The revelation could be a rehearsal for explaining it to Philip. If Mrs. Montgomery's response was to assume that Bridget had been to blame and was a loose woman, perhaps that was how Philip would react.

Bridget took a deep breath and began. " I was an indentured servant, and the doctor for whom I worked died. His brother took charge of everything. He was a horrid person and traumatized the whole household. One night, in a drunken rage, he attacked me, rendered me unconscious, and raped me. For that reason, I must tell Philip I am not the innocent girl he believes I am." Bridget began to weep.

"Oh my dear, how terrible. No wonder you have been so cautious around men. You saw Philip's anger at his brother for what he attempted to do. How do you think he would react to anyone raping you? You were unable to defend yourself against such a person. How could anyone think it was something you wanted to happen? You are the innocent victim here. Philip will understand, or he is not the man I believe him to be. If anything, he will be more gentle and careful with you." Mrs. Montgomery gave her a hug, a hanky, and a tiny glass of cordial.

Bridget hoped that Mrs. Montgomery was right. It would be better to speak to Philip as soon as possible. The longer she put it off, the worse it would be. She intended to visit Elizabeth that evening. If Philip were there, she would tell them both. The presence of his mother might give her courage.

Mrs. Montgomery had volunteered to go with Bridget to the de Palmer house, but Bridget felt that she needed to do it alone. Over and over, she practiced explaining everything.

Stepping down from the carriage, taking a deep breath, and straightening her shoulders, she marched up the steps. Bridget begged her angels for the strength to tell Philip what had happened and help him understand. Wearing a mask of confidence that she hoped hid the fear inside her heart, she rang the bell.

Lizzy was in the drawing room waiting for her. She was able to nod and smile. The smile was a little lopsided, but it was a smile. Bridget was delighted and hugged her. "You are making such progress. How wonderful." Elizabeth squeezed Bridget's hand. Philip appeared in the doorway.

"You see how well she is doing. She is always happy to see you, as am I." He kissed her hand and drew up a chair for her next to his mother. "You have been missed these last few days. We know that there are times when you are too busy to visit, but we are always delighted to see you." She felt her resolve fading. Bridget stood up and began to pace.

"There is something I must tell you. You have always been so kind and generous with your friendship, but there is something about me that you need to know." Philip started to speak, but Bridget stopped him."Please, this is hard enough. I must do this." She turned to face them.

Bridget told them everything. She paused and held her breath, waiting for their reaction. No one spoke, and her insides turned to ice. What had she done? When Bridget looked at Lizzy, tears were running down her cheeks. Philip stood staring at her, a look of horror on his face. Bridget turned and ran from the room. Philip caught her before she reached the front door.

"Oh my God, how could he have done such a thing? I can not imagine how much you suffered. You have kept this inside all this time? How brave you are. Will you ever trust a man again? Will you allow me to protect and care for you?"

Bridget began to cry, "I thought, by the look on your face, that you were repulsed by me." Philip put his arm around her and led her back to where his mother sat weeping.

"You silly goose, I was stunned. Just the thought of what that man...What had happened to you, what you had endured? I was trying to wrap my head around such brutality."

"I understand if you no longer wish to be my friend. I am not the innocent that you thought me to be."

"You are the innocent victim of a criminal act. That man should be hung."

Lizzy struggled to speak. "Hung," she managed to say, taking Bridget's hand and squeezing it.

"He is dead," Bridget stated, "He had a heart attack."

"That is probably a good thing, or I might have been charged with murder." Philip stood and rang the bell for the maid. "I would offer you a cordial, but there isn't any alcohol in the house. Let Ami bring us a cup of coffee. We need something before you leave. Will you be alright? Do you need me to see you home?"

"The carriage will be waiting for me. I didn't know how long I would be staying. Perhaps you would have sent me away after you heard my confession."

Chapter 47

Another Confession

Christmas was fast approaching. Trunks were being packed, and tickets had been purchased for the girls going home for the holidays. Invitations had been pouring in for parties. Most of society considered Philip and Bridget to be a couple. While some were critical of them, whispering behind their fans that Bridget wasn't or never would be in the same social class as Philip, Mrs. Montgomery said it was jealousy. Bridget didn't care what they thought; Philips's opinion was the only thing that mattered. As for Annabelle's opinion, she already knew the answer.

There was a small Christmas tree at the school, but the tree at the de Palmer house was spectacular. As dusk approached, the hundreds of tiny candles would be lit. The tree looked like something from a fairy tale. A beautiful angel with silvery wings and long, shiny hair graced the top. It took her breath away. A long-forgotten memory of the lady in the woods came flooding back.

She thought of the words that Isadora had uttered, "You are an extraordinary person." How long ago had she heard those words? How far she had come since then. "Thank you," she whispered.

Ever since the stroke, Bridget had prayed every night for the healing light to aid in Lizzy's recovery. Lizzy was making fantastic progress. The weakness on one side was hardly noticeable. If she spoke slowly, it was easy to understand her every word. She was delighted to think that Philip loved Bridget.

Mrs. Montgomery was the closest thing to family that Bridget had, so Philip had asked her permission to seek Bridget's hand in marriage. She had come to think of Bridget as a daughter and was delighted to know her prodigy would be making such a fine match. Not only was Philip a person of means, but someone who seemed to truly love Bridget. She happily gave her blessings to the union.

Before Philip could propose, he needed to tell Bridget something important. She had told him the story from her past, and now it was his turn.

"When I was a young man visiting my father's plantation, there was a slave girl that I was fond of. She became pregnant, and I asked my father to free her. He laughed and threatened to sell her. My uncle, my mentor and benefactor, purchased her and took her to Boston. Papers were drawn up to prove she was a free woman, but she died birthing my son. I have taken care of the boy ever since. He is smart, and I made sure that he had an excellent education. I have never denied that Lucus is my son, but I am aware of the problems associated with being a person of mixed race in this country. He is at a university in France and will be involved in running my European company someday. It was important for you to be aware of this because it might alter our relationship. I am in love with you and would ask you to be my wife, but I will not deny my son. You need time to think about this. Do not answer now. We can talk about this in a day or two."

After Philip left, Bridget sat there mulling over everything he had said. Philip had a grown illegitimate son of mixed blood. Philip loved her and wanted to marry her. The only thing that should matter was their love for each other and whether or not she could be the wife he deserved. The fact that he cared about and provided for his illegitimate son only made Bridget love him more.

Chapter 48

A Terrible Night.

The New Year had come and gone. Philip had given Bridget the most glorious betrothal ring, and she couldn't stop staring at it in disbelief. She thought back to a time when she had vowed never to marry.

Philip had been so patient. How long would he wait? His gentle kisses made her long for more, but then the fear would raise its ugly head, and she would panic. Would there ever come a time when she could be Philip's wife in the true sense of the word?

Bridget was sleeping soundly. Shouts and gunfire woke her. She threw on a wrap and ran barefoot to the big house. Just as she reached the sitting room, the front door burst open. A group of men carrying wooden cudgels, rifles, and whips stormed in. Mrs. Montgomery was standing in the middle of the room. The men began shouting at her, accusing her of harboring a runaway slave.

"How dare you break into my house. I had just finished preparing the curriculum for the next semester and was about to retire. How could I possibly be involved with the things you are accusing me of? Do you see any slaves here?"

"We saw the boy run in this direction. A woman was helping him. Search the house. He couldn't have gone far. We shot at the pair. I think we wounded one."

"You have permission to search my house, even if you were so rude that you chose not to ask for it. Thank goodness my students are not in residence. Your actions would have frightened them and perhaps caused me to lose them. When you are finished, I do expect an apology. I have been a respected member of society in Charlotte for many years."

Bridget could not believe her eyes. She stood staring at the men as they swarmed over the house, opening anything that could have hidden a young boy. She turned to ask Mrs.Montgomery if there was anything she could do to help A bloody stain on the bodice of her mentor caught her eye. She watched in horror as it slowly spread across her back. Bridget reached for the shawl on the couch and wrapped it around Mrs. Montgomery's shoulders, making sure it covered the damming evidence.

It seemed as if the hunt went on for hours, but at last, the group returned sheepishly to where the two women stood. Hat in hand, the leader said he must have been mistaken. The slave must have slipped away in the dark.

Philip arrived at the front door in time to see the last of the men depart."What the hell happened? I hear the noise from blocks away. What happened? Are you both alright?" He hadn't stopped to put on his coat, and his shirt was half-buttoned. He caught Mrs. Montgomery as she began to faint and gently sat her on the couch. "Shut the door and dim the lamp." she managed to whisper. She lifted her hoop skirt to reveal the young black boy hiding there.

"She is wounded. "Bridget said, "She is bleeding."

"I was running so fast. Something stung, but I didn't know I was hit. Is the boy alright? We need to get him to safety." Mrs. Montgomery tried to stand.

"We will, but first, we must take care of your wound." Philip took the boy into the library, drew the heavy curtains, and said, "Stay here and be quiet. We will find a way to get you away safely, but they will be looking everywhere for you. It would be too risky to do anything tonight. Now, I must take care of the brave woman who risked her life to save you."

Philip returned to the sitting room. Bridget had unfastened the back of the dress and was carefully cleaning the wound. The bullet had only grazed the skin. A pressure bandage would take care of it. Mrs. Montgomery would be in pain for a week or two, but there wasn't much harm done.

"What were you thinking? You could have been killed. Don't you know what that mob would have done to you if they knew you were helping a runaway slave? You put both yourself and Bridget in terrible danger." Philip said, pouring three whiskeys. "I will stay here tonight to be sure you are safe. Tomorrow, I will have the lock on the front door repaired. Do you have a firearm in the house?" He passed each of the ladies a glass and urged them to drink. "This will help steady your nerves. You both have had a nasty shock. Bridget, I would ask you to stay in the big house tonight for safety. There are bands of enraged men roaming the streets. Most of them have been drinking."

Mrs. Montgomery handed him the keys to the large cabinet containing her late husband's gun collection. While the guns hadn't been fired in a while, they appeared to be in working condition. After loading them, Philip placed them on the table. "These will do for tonight. Tomorrow, I will clean them and show you how to use them. It is something that you both should know. Dangerous times are coming."

Even with the whiskey's help, it took a while for the two women to fall asleep on the couch. Philip had embraced Bridget and held her close. "I am glad you're safe," he whispered. He moved an oversized chair to where he had a clear view of the door. The sound of the mob had moved off into the distance, but Philip wasn't taking any chances. He remained there until morning.

Chapter 49

How It Happened

The next morning, Mrs. Montgomery explained how the incident the night before had happened. She was an adviser to the local primary school board and had been at the meeting at the church. She wasn't aware that the preacher was a member of the Underground Railroad, an organization that aided runaway slaves escaping to the North. The boy had come to the church expecting it to be empty but found it filled with people.

Leaving the meeting, she became aware of a group of men searching the woods near the church. Looking around, she pretended to rebuckle her shoe. That was when she discovered the young black boy hiding under the steps. Mrs. Montgomery seized his hand, pulled him up, and whispered, "Come with me now. Walk fast, and don't look around."

They had managed to cover quite a bit of ground before the men spotted them. Thank God they didn't have the bloodhounds with them, or all would have been lost. The two of them ran as fast as possible, with the mob chasing them. Shots were fired. They squeezed through the fence, ran up the stairs, and were in the house before the gang could be sure where they had gone. There was no time to find a safe place to hide the slave. The men were right behind them. The boy curled up in a tight ball, and Mrs. Montgomery dropped her hoop skirt over him and turned to greet the men as they burst through the door.

Several days later, a cart delivered a load of firewood to the house. The driver emptied the cart, then carefully removed a few boards from the floor, exposing a hidden compartment. Having received payment for the wood, he drove away. The boy Mrs. Montgomery had rescued was on his way to freedom. It would be a long and perilous journey, but prayers were said for his safe arrival.

Philip was concerned for Martha, as Mrs. Montgomery had asked him to call her. Anyone who was found to have aided runaways was in danger.

"I had never done anything like that before, but I couldn't let them hang the boy. He had interfered when their master raped his sister. All he did was try to protect her. Why are people so cruel? I grew up thinking there was nothing wrong with owning slaves. Everyone I knew owned them. Now, I am beginning to wonder if it's right. I am so glad my husband gave ours their freedom."

"I agree with you, but speaking of these things openly is unwise. It is not a popular idea in Charlotte. If the rumors about the leanings of the northern congress and who will become the next president turn out to be true, there is talk of succession. Slaves are what the economy is based on in the South. It would collapse without them. People are either for or against slavery. There is no middle ground. I fear this smoldering idea will burst into a dangerous blaze sooner or later." Philip shook his head. "It could pit brother against brother."

Chapter 50

There Were Rumors.

Bridget had returned to her tiny house to collect a few things. She had decided Philip was right, and she would sleep in the big house for safety. There was more than enough room with the students away for the holiday. As much as she had respected her mentor before that night, Mrs. Montgomery's bravery in the face of danger had increased her admiration a thousandfold. Bridget was amazed at the quick thinking that had saved the boy's life from a rabid mob, perhaps even their own lives.

Something else strange had taken place that night. When Philip had held her close, the heat of his skin against the thin fabric of her nightdress seemed to scald her. For hours after and even the next morning, she could feel it.

It was her reaction that surprised Bridget. She tried to tell herself that it was the aftermath of the dangerous situation they had been in, but she knew it was something more. Her body had responded to his embrace. Instead of the usual fear that would cause her to pull back, there was a need, a want... She wanted him to hold her close, to feel his naked skin against hers. Finally, she understood the desire women whispered about. Did this mean that she could be a wife to Philip in the true sense of the word? Only time would tell, but she sang as she helped straighten up the mess from the previous night.

True to his promise, Philip checked and cleaned the guns, showing both women how to load, aim, and fire the weapons. He took them out to a field far from town, set up bottles, and had them shoot at the targets until he felt they stood a fair chance of defending themselves. More practice would be required, but this would have to do for now. Beelzebub would be spending nights with the women for their safety. The dog was as content to be with Bridget as with Philip.

Bridget noticed that the visitations and the invitations were not as plentiful as they had been. From time to time, she would catch some of the ladies whispering to each other, but when they saw her listening, they quickly turned away. The story of the runaway slave had been passed around. While no one could say if Mrs. Montgomery had been involved in the escape, there were rumors. Persons who were not second or third-generation southerners were looked on with suspicion now.

Chapter 51

Planning a Wedding.

Bridget had been preparing her trousseau. Their bans had been posted, and the wedding day was fast approaching. Trunks had been packed and labeled for the trip to France in September. Philip's mother and Beelzebub would stay with Mrs. Montgomery while they were gone.

That had been the plan. Now Philip was having second thoughts about leaving. The South was becoming a tinder box. It would only take a spark to set the whole country ablaze. He couldn't take the chance of leaving his mother and Mrs. Montgomery unprotected. People were becoming irrational. Anything could happen. Crowds gathered to witness lynchings. It had become a spectator sport. The genteel, courteous South had disappeared, and in its place was a rabid mob.

Bridget agreed. As wonderful as it would have been to see France and to meet Philip's son, to leave those they loved unprotected would be a constant worry. They would be too far away to help if anything happened. Philip wasn't sure he could count on his brothers to do the right thing. If things settled down, they could take the trip later. Philip laughed, saying, "They had the rest of their lives to do that."

Mary and her husband were planning to come to Charlotte for the wedding. Bridget could hardly believe her friend was making the long trip to be there. Mrs. Montgomery would give her away, and Mary would be her maid of honor. Her eyes filled with tears of gratitude whenever she thought about it all. What had she ever done to deserve such happiness?

The reception was to be held in the ballroom at the big house. An enormous double-layered cake and crates of champagne had been ordered. Invitations had been sent, musicians had been selected, and extra help had been hired.

Her wedding dress had belonged to Philip's mother. Bridget had never seen anything so beautiful. Mrs. Montgomery had given her a pearl necklace that had been in the family for generations. Mary had sent her a nightdress trimmed with Italian lace in a soft shade of lavender for the honeymoon. The past few weeks, she had surprised and delighted Philip with her eagerness when he kissed her. How could her life be any better?

Chapter 52

A Change of Plans

How fast plans can change Lincoln had been put forward as a presidential candidate, and now the call for succession rang out loud and clear. There would be a gathering of South Carolina politicians and leaders to discuss where they would go from here. The school teacher had been tarred and feathered and sent away in disgrace. While there hadn't been any proof of his involvement in the Underground Railroad, that didn't matter. Just the suspicion of his actions had been enough. Things were quickly getting out of hand.

Mary and her husband were Quakers. The sect had been openly anti-slavery and actively helped slaves flee to freedom. For the couple to come to Charlotte now would be to put their lives in danger. They could end up in jail, or worse, Bridget understood why Mary couldn't stand up with her, but it was a huge disappointment.

To make matters worse, many had declined the wedding invitation, and others were openly hostile. Bridget tried to put all these things aside. The important thing was that soon, she would be Philips's wife. While Philip's family were plantation owners, people considered Philip an outsider. His business was located in the North, and he had lived there for years.

Philip had been carefully transferring his monies to northern banks for the last six months. His solicitors had quietly sold the majority of his southern holdings, and he had encouraged Mrs. Montgomery to do the same. With all the talk of succession, it was the smart thing to do. If trouble came, they would be prepared.

Philip had been at his lawyer's making specific arrangements. He returned home to find a cross had been burned in front of his house. His mother had stepped out to protest. Beelzebub had joined her. Sensing her fear, the dog attacked the hooded men who stood cursing and shouting vulgar epitaphs. Someone pulled a gun and fired several shots before running off. Philip's mother was kneeling by the dying dog, blood and tears staining her dress.

Chapter 53

A Sad Farewell.

Mrs. Montgomery had left days earlier. Her students would not be returning, so the school was closed. Perhaps she would create another in Boston or New York. Philip agreed it was the most prudent thing to do. He, too, was preparing to leave Charlotte. The problem was his mother. Lizzy refused to go. This was her home, and here she would stay.

After the terrible incident with the burning cross and the death of Beelzebub, he felt sure she would be willing to leave. He had called on the police to find the men who had perpetrated the deed, but they didn't seem eager to pursue the matter. Perhaps their friends had been involved, or worse, they had been part of the mob.

Bridget and Philip spent hours trying to persuade her. The South was headed down a dangerous path. No matter how they begged and pleaded, Lizzy stood her ground. She was too old to go traipsing around to strange places. The South was her home, and she would be buried there next to her husband.

His older brother wasn't of any use in the matter. He believed the South was in the right and would prevail against the North. His mother would be welcome to return to the plantation. No harm could come to her there and Elizabeth was sure the plantation was the safest place to be.

The house servants Philip had purchased had been given papers declaring them free persons of color and sent north with Mrs. Montgomery. Elizabeth's lady's maid had also been offered her freedom. She chose to stay, stating that she had been with her mistress for many years and wouldn't desert her now. Philip explained that he had left papers with his solicitor for her. The monies and papers would be her path to freedom if and when she needed them.

Hugs and tearful farewells had taken place. Elizabeth's bags, favorite chair, and bed were placed on a cart to be sent on ahead. Annabelle came to fetch her mother-in-law and the maid. With a triumphant smile, Annabelle helped Lizzy into the carriage, and then, without a wave or backward glance, Annabelle drove away.

The division between the North and South was growing. Other states were considering succession. A law had been passed allowing bounty hunters to track and return slaves seeking refuge in the North. The bounty hunters were not too careful about who they brought back. Some were free men and not slaves. That didn't matter to them. If you were black, you were fair game.

Bridget thought back to a time when her life had seemed perfect. Had that only been weeks ago? How could things go so wrong so fast? Now, her whole world was in turmoil. Beelzebub was dead, Elizabeth was gone, her wedding was in limbo, and she and Philip appeared to be outcasts.

It was time to leave. Trunks had been sent north to Philip's home. He had been at the dock to procure an earlier sailing date. He had booked three berths on a ship leaving for France on the next high tide. The ship captain could marry them, and a priest in France would sanctify the marriage. Soon, he and Bridget would be man and wife.

Philip had planned for his mother to sail with them. Elizabeth would be safer away from the South, and it was time for her to meet her grandson, but that was not to be. Once again, she refused to leave. Philip's fear was that he would never see his mother again.

Chapter 54

A Voyage and a Visit

The crossing was amazingly calm for that time of year. What a difference from the last time Bridget had been on a ship. She had been in the ship's bowels with little food, water, and too many people. Now, she was in a first-class cabin, dining at the captain's table and strolling on the deck when weather permitted. It all seemed like a fairy tale.

Bridget stood by the rail, gazing out at the sea. Soon, she and Philip would be going in for supper. Later, they would return to their cabin. Her heart beat faster, thinking of what the night would bring. She was Mrs. Philip de Palmer. At first, Philip was careful not to frighten her, taking his time and following her lead. His patience had paid off. Bridget was eager to retire to the bedroom. How afraid she had been, but now their lovemaking took her breath away.

From time to time, she would mourn the loss of her brave Beelzebub. She missed her faithful companion. Elizabeth was also on her mind. She was aware of Philip's concern for his mother's well-being. These were the only things that marred the happiness she felt. Bridget was sailing into a new life, in a new country, as a new bride. They would be returning to an

America in conflict, but until then, this was their honeymoon, and they would make the best of it.

It was a cold, rainy morning when they landed in France. Philip pointed out that England was just across the channel. When Bridget left Ireland years ago, she could never have foreseen this. All that was needed was a quick trip on a ferry, and she would be home. If foolish enough to do that, would she be able to find her sisters? Would they even remember who she was? That part of her life had been over for years. There was no need to dredge it up.

Their luggage was loaded on the coach that would take them to Paris. Reservations had been made at the Hotel Grande, and Philip's son would be waiting for them. After spending a week in Paris, they would move on to the Riviera, where it would be warmer. Philip would take care of some business while in France, but the nights would belong to them alone. Bridget sometimes felt as if she would wake up and find it all had been an impossible dream. Was she truly the wife of Philip de Palmer?

The rain was coming down harder when they arrived at the hotel. Bridget was glad to pass through the doors and into the warm lobby with its blazing fire. A tall, handsome man with dark curly hair and hazel eyes stood with his back to the flames. When he saw Philip, he hurried over and flung his arms around his father. He bent over, kissed Bridget's hand, and welcomed her to Paris in the most perfect French. Philip was beaming with pride, and Bridget could see why. This was an exceptional young man. His grandmother would have fallen in love with him at first sight.

They awoke the following day to brilliant sunshine. Paris had been freshly washed and was a sight to behold. Lucus had arrived with a bouquet for Bridget. He had ordered a carriage and was prepared to proudly show them his adopted city.

Philip had asked that they first stop at a well-known furrier. Once there, he explained that he wished to purchase a stole for his wife. Bridget was overwhelmed by the selection of beautiful furs. She protested, saying, "There was no need for anything so expensive." Philip laughed, kissed her, then draped the best, the most elegant stole around her shoulders, stating, "The last thing I want is for my bride to catch a cold on her honeymoon." Lucus smiled, "French women are known for being elegant. They can not hold a candle to you."

The carriage ride was wonderful. Next, they took a walk through the Tulleries Gardens. The fall air was filled with fragrance. Soon, the cold blast of winter would cause the blooms to die, but for now, they were showing off. The gardens were perfect, the city was perfect, and Bridget declared the whole day perfect. It was dark, and the wind had picked up by the time they returned to the hotel, tired but happy. That night was the first night since they had married that they fell asleep without making love.

Philip had explained their situation and convinced a priest to marry them again. The amount of silver offered for the service helped. Lucus stood with them as they retook their vows. He kissed her and called her "Mamma." Bridget was overwhelmed. How could life get any better?

Chapter 55

Farewell to France

The week in Paris had flown by. Every day had been filled with the city's sights, sounds, tastes, and smells—unlike anything Bridget had ever experienced. Once again, she wondered if she would wake up to find this was only a beautiful dream.

Lucus was as charming as his father and had his father's business savvy. The head of the European branch spoke highly of his knowledge and commitment. Philip was filled with pride. The business would be in good hands when Lucus was old enough to take over.

It was Nov. 1860, and Lincoln had been elected president of the United States of America. The news of the election had reached France, as well as the fact that the southern states were succeeding one after the other. No one could predict what would happen next, but a war between the states seemed imminent. Philip was concerned for his family and his firm in America. The visit to the south of France must wait. He booked passage on the Persia, the fastest ship ever made. They would be in New York in less than two weeks.

The voyage back to America was horrid. While the trip to France had been calm, the rough seas and scary storms kept them confined to their cabins. The ship labored through the huge waves and threatened to lose power as water swamped the engine room. At last, New York appeared on the horizon.

It was cold in New York. Bridget was grateful for the fur that Philip had insisted they buy in Paris. He had warmer clothing, dresses, and more brought to the hotel for her approval. She would need them because Boston would be just as cold and windy. A few days later, they left for his home.

Because they were not expected to return for several weeks, the house had not been aired out, nor had fires been laid. The housekeeper quickly set a fire in the bedroom fireplace and placed warming pans in the bed. A meal was brought in from a nearby restaurant, and they ate it picnic-style on the bedroom rug. Hopefully, the entire staff would arrive in time to prepare breakfast in the morning.

When she awoke, Bridget felt a little off-kilter with the time change. It took a moment to remember where she was, and there was no sign of Philip. She was preparing to leave the warm bed and look for him when there was a knock, and a maid entered with a tray.

"My name is Sara. I have brought you some hot coffee, Madam, with cream and sugar if you wish. First, let me freshen up the fire. It's cold in here. Would Madam prefer breakfast in bed or in the dining room?"

Having poked a toe out from the covers, Bridget quickly decided to remain in bed till the room warmed up. Sara placed the tray on the bed, fluffed the pillows, and wrapped a shawl around Bridget's shoulders.

"Mr. Philip has gone to the office. You are to have lunch and rest until he returns. He will be back in time to take you out for dinner. Your trunks were sent from Charlotte several weeks ago. I took the liberty of hanging up your gowns and putting away your things. I will be happy to rearrange them if they are not to your liking."

"This hot coffee is perfect. Thank you, Sara. I'm sure whatever you did with the dresses is fine, but could you find my dressing gown so I may get up later?"

"Yes, Madam, Would you like some toast with jam or something more substantial? Unfortunately, the cook has not arrived as yet, but I could fix eggs and ham."

"Toast will be just what I need. Thank you, Sara." Bridget snuggled down in the cozy covering and sipped the hot coffee. She would make an effort to get up in a little while, but it was so lovely and warm where she was, and she had nowhere to go and nothing to do. Perhaps she would take a nap. How wonderfully decadent she felt.

Chapter 56

A Cold Reception

Winter in the north was a new experience for Bridget. She had suffered from the cold and damp in Ireland, but now she had spent too many years in the south. Her blood had thinned out. She found it much nicer to stay home by a roaring fire. A light supper with Philip suited her better than the dinner parties with too many people and rooms filled with cigar smoke. They made her nauseous. The conversations among the men were about trade, money, and the outbreak of the war. The women gossiped about people Bridget didn't know and ignored her completely.

Young men on either side were learning how to kill other young men. They bravely went off to fight, thinking it was the thing to do. They had no understanding of the horrors they faced. The toys that appealed to males before they experienced the battlefield for themselves were uniforms, swords, and guns. Once they found themselves in the midst of war, it was too late.

Bridget hated the thought of the country being torn apart. She loved the South with its slower, more genteel way of life. On the other hand, the people of Boston seemed less friendly, always in a hurry, and cold in more ways than one.

The majority of wives married to Philip's aquatints viewed her as an outsider and saw no reason to include her at any social event. They made no secret of their feelings toward her, calling her "the Southerner." She had invited them to an afternoon tea, and because their husbands had insisted, they came, but Bridget would never try that again.

Soon, there was another reason to remain at home. Bridget became aware of the cause of her nausea. She was with child. Philip would have a second son or perhaps a daughter. He couldn't believe their luck. A room was to be converted into a nursery.

A week later, Bridget woke in great pain. Her nightdress and bed were covered in blood. The doctor was called, but there was nothing that could be done. She had lost the baby, and the doctor informed them there was little chance of her ever carrying a child. Philip insisted they didn't need to take his word for it. A specialist might have a different diagnosis. Bridget was inconsolable. How happy she had been to be carrying Philip's baby.

Chapter 57

A Friend to the Rescue.

Bridget remembered her mother's depression and the terrible results, but there were days when just getting out of bed was an effort. She knew Philip was worried, so she tried to pull herself out of the bottomless pit she was in. Weeks went by, but still, she felt dead inside. The only thing that helped was the pain draft the doctor had prescribed. Finally, Philip sent for Mrs. Montgomery.

Martha arrived and took control of the situation. She, too, had lost a child and understood what Bridget was going through. "Doctors are not always right, but if you continue to do nothing to help with your recovery and if you continue with these opioids, you will make their predictions come true. It is time to stop wallowing in your grief. Philip, too, has lost a child. Do you want him to lose his wife as well?" She made Bridget get up and get dressed. Mrs. Montgomery insisted she write letters to Mary and Abigail and take a walk every day. A piano teacher was brought in to give her lessons. Martha Montgomery was a strict taskmaster who made sure that Bridget practiced daily. She was still grieving, but slowly, Bridget joined the living once more.

Martha suggested that Philip purchase a puppy from the same breeder as Beelzebub. It would give Bridget something to take care of. Still grieving the loss of her child, Bridget wasn't sure she was ready for a dog. The loss of Beelzebub had been heart-wrenching, but she melted when "Bella" licked her hand and begged to be picked up. The pup was a miniature of her forerunner, except for a white blaze on her forehead. Bella's paws indicated just how large she would be, but for now, she fit perfectly in Bridget's lap.

Chapter 58

Jhon.

Bridget loved walking the dog. It was late spring, the weather was perfect, and the exercise was good for them. Unfortunately, on one of their excursions, a young boy snatched Bridget's purse. Bella, who by this time was half-grown, knocked the boy to the ground and stood over him.

A passing policeman picked the child up and was about to arrest him when he began to cry. "My mom is sick, and there is no food. My sister is hungry. All I wanted was money for food."

Bridget remembered when she had been the one trying to feed her siblings. "The boy is fine. I will take him to buy food and bring it to his family, officer." Then, she turned to the young thief and said, " If you wish to take care of your family, you will help me."

He stared at her, trying to decide what to do. He could run away after they had purchased something for his mother and sister to eat, so for now, he would go with her and her big dog.

Bridget bought bread, eggs, tea, and ham. She gave the boy the basket to carry but attached the dog's leash to the handle to prevent him from running off with it. Jhon had no choice but to return home.

The family was housed in one room. Jhon's mother lay on a pallet on the floor. She attempted to rise when she realized they had a visitor. His sister sat on the floor sucking her thumb, but when she saw the dog, she squealed with delight and threw her skinny little arms around Bella's neck.

Begging Jhon's mother to rest, Bridget set about preparing tea and slicing the bread and ham. The woman drank the tea but ate little. Jhon and his sister gobbled down the sandwiches so fast that Bridget was afraid they would make themselves sick.

Bridget was not yet entirely well, and now she felt the extra effort she had put in since beginning her walk. She sent Jhon out to hail a carriage and driver. While Bridget waited, Jhon's mother explained that they had arrived from Holland several years ago, but her husband had been killed on the job, and her work as a washerwoman had come to an end when she became ill. There was no money for food or rent. The church across the way from their dwelling prepared a soup for the hungry when it could, but times were hard for Saint Gregory as well.

When the carriage came, and after promising to return, an exhausted Bridget and Bella returned home to be met by a worried Philip. He had been ready to send out a search party to find his missing wife.

Philip realized that for the first time in a long time, his wife's interest in Jhon's family gave her a sense of purpose. Bridget had a new lease on life, but he was concerned for her safety when visiting such a neighborhood. Philip donated significantly to Saint Gregory's church to aid in their food distribution, and Bridget promised never to go there without Bella and the security offered by Philips's driver.

Chapter 59

A Deadly Fire.

Jhon's sister Catherine blossomed with Bridget's care, but her mother continued to decline. There were no visible signs of an illness, just a day-by-day weakening. Vomiting followed any food she could be enticed to eat. Even the tea seldom stayed down. John was her constant caregiver. Bridget understood only too well the stress he was under.

The last day of spring brought a sudden storm. Bridget had arrived home soaked to her skin, and by that evening, she was coughing and running a high fever. The doctor was called. A week's bed rest, soup, and teas were ordered. Bridget was devastated. Who would take care of Jhon and his family? Philip assured her his driver was familiar with their needs and would handle the deliveries until she was better.

A week had passed, and soon Bridget would be able to make the deliveries herself. The driver always stopped by each evening to give her the latest news about the family. She appreciated his interest but couldn't wait to see them for herself.

One evening, the driver was running late. Bridget became concerned. When he did arrive hours later, he was covered in soot and visibly upset. Philip sat him down and gave him a stiff drink.

Tears running down his face, the driver explained, "I arrived to find everything in flames. The boy had carried his little sister to safety. I put her in the carriage and turned to help, but it was too late. He had gone back for his mother. By then, several of the buildings were on fire. Firemen worked to douse the flames, but there was no sign of the boy or his mother. They found the bodies lying together in the doorway. He died trying to save her. The little girl was coughing and having difficulty breathing, so I took her to the hospital. The doctors said it was from breathing the smoke. They will keep her tonight. She keeps calling for Jhon. I couldn't tell her he was gone."

Bridget was unable to speak. Jhon and his mother were gone. How could that be and Catherine was in the hospital? They must go to her immediately. The exhausted driver offered to drive them, but Philip thanked him and sent him home.

They arrived at the hospital and were taken to where Catherine lay sleeping, the tears drying on her cheeks. The doctor explained she had been so distraught and calling for her brother that she had been given a sleeping draught to calm her. She had breathed in smoke, but thanks to her brother, the amount had been minimal. Her lungs would clear with no real damage.

Philip assured the hospital that the costs would be covered and she must have the best care. Her brother's death was not to be spoken of, and they would return in the morning to take her home.

Chapter 60

An Unbelievable Turn of Events.

Philip and Bridget brought Catherine home. She spent days in tears after learning of her brother's and mother's death. The only thing that comforted her was Bella's presence. The dog seemed to understand that the little girl needed her and became her constant companion.

Catherine would have nightmares about the fire and wake up screaming. The dog became her bedmate. As the weeks passed, the bad dreams faded away, and the little girl began to smile again, but Bella refused to give up her place in Catherine's bed.

Philip had made inquiries about whether there were any family members who could care for the girl. None were found. He had checked with the parish priest, who knew something about the family, but it wasn't much. They had immigrated to America several years before, and the little girl was born and baptized shortly after. She would be about three. To his knowledge, there were no relatives.

That had not been the only inquiry Philip had made. Unknown to Bridget, a search had occurred earlier in Ireland for Bridget's sisters. They had been difficult to find, but at last, he located them both.

Her eldest sister was happily married and wanted nothing to do with Bridget, whom she felt had abandoned her. The pregnant younger sister had been widowed. She had been corresponding with Philip's solicitor concerning a voyage to America. Unfortunately, she had died in childbirth before anything was settled.

The baby, a boy, had been placed in an orphanage. Philip had a lawyer looking into the prospect of adopting him. He had said nothing to Bridget about finding her sisters or the adoption until he was sure such a thing was possible. He didn't want to disappoint her if his efforts failed.

Catherine had become an integral part of their household. Bridget couldn't bear to think of the house without the little girl. In her heart, she secretly wished no family members existed.

The child had found her voice and chattered like a magpie. She would dress Bella in a bonnet and make her sit and play tea party. Bridget loved her as if she were her own.

Philip had received the reply from Ireland that he had been hoping for. Bridget's nephew could be adopted by his aunt. It was time for him to share his findings.

Philip sat Bridget down and told her of his quest. Knowing how sad she had been over losing her sisters so many years ago, he had searched for them, and the search had proved fruitful.

When Bridget heard of her youngest sister's death and the baby boy who had survived both of his parents, she wept. Philip explained how he had ascertained through his lawyers that it would be possible for them to adopt the child. Once more, she couldn't stop crying, but they were tears of joy.

Philip sailed to Ireland to sign the papers that would officially make him a father for the second time. He hired a wet nurse to accompany him and care for the baby on the trip back.

Bridget waited at home, not daring to believe she would soon be the mother of a baby boy. Before he left, she and Philip had petitioned the court for permission to adopt Catherine. Bridget had lost all hope of ever having children, but now she would have two. They decided to call the boy Jhon, after Catherine's brother. Without his sacrifice, they wouldn't have their daughter.

Chapter 61

Changes and Sad News

Going from a childless home to one filled with children was a big change. The wet nurse had stayed on to feed and care for Jhon. The baby was a bundle of delight. Catherine adored her brother, and Bridget counted her blessings every day. Mrs. Montgomery had purchased a house nearby and happily played the role of grandmother.

Even though he had been raised and educated in the North, Philip had lost several clients. They judged him by his Southern roots. He had also refused to purchase stock in munition factories. While he believed the South was wrong, he wasn't willing to provide the means to kill Southern soldiers. There was still more than enough income to support his family.

An old black woman appeared at his office. He recognized her as his mother's maid. She had acquired the papers he had left for her at the solicitor's office and managed to flee from the plantation after his mother's death. She had come north for her safety and to tell him of his mother's passing.

Lizzy had died peacefully in her sleep and, thankfully, hadn't lived to see her beloved home burned to the ground by Union soldiers. She had been buried next to her husband in the family cemetery. His brothers were off somewhere fighting for the South, and his sister-in-law had left earlier with a carriage full of valuables. What she couldn't carry, she had buried in the garden. The maid had no idea where she had gone.

Philip thanked her for her service and gave her money to help her make her way to Canada. That would be the safest place for her now.

After she had gone, Philip sat there deep in thought. His mother had never met his oldest son, and now she would never know her newest grandchildren. How much his mother would have loved cuddling Jhon and playing dress-up with Catherine. Philip had loved his mother with all her flaws. He closed the office early and went home to share the loss of Lizzy with her daughter-in-law.

Chapter 62

A Political Choice

Even with the added concern for her new family, Bridget and Mrs. Montgomery made an effort to change the lives of the people in Jhon's old neighborhood. They contacted the more prosperous churches and convinced them to help with the soup kitchens. Many of the men were off fighting, and families were left without any means of support.

Philip spoke to the city council about the building permits issued in these neighborhoods. Fires were a constant threat. The chances of these fires occurring because of the poor construction and shoddy materials being used were obvious. These fires might not stay confined but could easily spread to the more affluent areas. It would be in the city's best interest to change the laws. Boston should set an example of how a city protects all its citizens, rich and poor. The new ordinance was passed unanimously.

The work done by the de Palmer family and friends did not go unnoticed. Philip interested his business acquaintances and even some bankers in funding an agency to oversee poor children's education and raise the age at which they could be put to work. He saw to it that a list of the contributors was posted monthly in the paper. This publicity didn't hurt his cause a bit.

The next election found Philip's name on the list for city council. Two years later, he became the mayor of Boston. The war had finally turned in favor of the North. A blockade of southern ports meant that the South had lost its primary source of income. The North had become industrialized over the years, so while times were hard there, it was nothing like the suffering the Confederacy was experiencing.

Because Philip had business connections in Uta, the government sent him with a proposition. He was to ensure that Uta would take no sides in the conflict and that the railroad would be allowed to continue traveling through that state with the supplies needed to reinforce the Union army. There were concessions made on both sides, but Uta remained neutral. This deal was an important part of the war effort, and Philip had made essential allies in Washington.

Chapter 63

Sad News

Lincoln had been re-elected for a second term, and the war was finally drawing to a close. Philip sent out requests seeking information about his brothers. It would be months before he received the news he was dreading.

His older brother had died in a Union prison camp during the second year of the war. The whereabouts of his younger brother had been more challenging to ascertain. The news, when it came, was even harder to hear.

Annabelle had taken up with a Union officer and lived comfortably in Winchester in the Shenandoah Valley until the South once again recaptured the city. The citizens took it upon themselves to lock her up and charge her with collaborating with the enemy. Nathan had been with the liberating Confederate army. When he discovered Annabelle's plight, he left his unit and returned to help her. He was caught, charged with desertion and aiding an enemy of the state. He was tried and hung. Annabelle disappeared, and no one knew her whereabouts. If Philip found her, he would hang her himself.

Bridget knew her sister-in-law wasn't nice but found it hard to believe she had been responsible for Nathans's death. Annabelle seemed able to escape the consequences of any trouble she had created. All thoughts of revenge on Annabelle were forgotten with the news of Lincoin's assassination. The whole country was in shock and morning.

Chapter 64

A Dreadful Revelation.

Several years later, Philip's meteoric rise saw him proposed as the next governor of Massachusetts. If elected, Bridget would be his First Lady. She and Mrs. Montgomery had once again opened a school for young girls. The profits were used to fund a school in the poorer part of town. How much would their lives change if Philip was elected?

Jhon and Catherine were both in school. Bridget and Philip could never remember a time when the children had not been a part of their lives. Jhon was a redheaded ball of energy that had been reading since the age of three. Catherine was a piano prodigy with an amazing voice. Would the children need to leave the school they loved?

As governor, Philip would be able to do even more for the people of Massachusetts. That was important, but so was their family. These things must be considered. Bridget wasn't sure she wanted to be the wife of a governor. It would be like living in a goldfish bowl.

There was to be a rally where Philip would officially declare his candidacy. If this was what he wanted, Bridget would support him. They stood together on the podium. His accomplishments were spoken of, and the audience applauded each and every one. He was about to speak when a woman in the crowd called out.

"What about your wife? She appears to be a fine lady. Of course, no one would know she was Irish and came to this country as an indentured servant. How did she lose her Irish brogue, become a school teacher, a southern belle, and marry into the de Palmer family? What other secrets is she hiding?"

Philip wished to answer, but Bridget stopped him. "How kind of you. Rather than spreading stories with subtle innuendos or half-truths, you have chosen to do it in such a public manner," she said. "Yes, I am Irish. I lost my family, saw my brother shot, and left my home for a new country. After weeks in the bowels of a ship, I arrived in America as an indentured servant. I understand what it is to be poor and desperate. With the help of kind, understanding people, I gained my freedom, received an education, and became a teacher. My husband knew of my humble beginnings and chose to marry me anyway. I am proud of all my husband has accomplished, and if elected, I can assure you Philip de Palmer will continue to make Massachusetts a great place to live for all her citizens."

Her speech was met with thunderous applause and a standing ovation. Philip laughed and declared that if she ran for governor against him, she would undoubtedly win.

Some of Philips's supporters tried to escort the women out. Instead, she shouted, "That's not the only secret this couple is hiding. Ask Philip about his bastard son. He has a black illegitimate son. Ask him." There were audible gasps from the crowd. While Philip had never made an effort to keep Lucus's existence a secret, most people were unaware he had a child out of wedlock and that his son was colored.

Philip understood his chances of becoming governor had just gone up in smoke. While most Northerners were proud of their stance against slavery, they were not broad-minded enough to accept this new revelation. His hope of earning any public office, even dog catcher, was dashed.

Philip was curious about the speaker's identification. She seemed to know a lot of things that were not common knowledge. He would have a detective look into it. The answer soon became apparent.

Annabelle had arrived in Boston hoping to cause trouble. Her hatred of Bridget and Philip had festered for years, and now she sought revenge. Philip's anger rose as he remembered all the pain she had caused his family, including the death of his younger brother.

As long as she remained in the North, she was safe. Was there any way to return her to a Southern prison? A Southern court had convicted her as a collaborator. Did the sentence still stand? Annabelle had never paid for any trouble she caused. Maybe there was a way to change that. Philip was determined to find it.

Chapter 65

The Ambassador's Wife

Philip contacted a colleague in Washington who owed him a favor to inquire about Annabelle's status as an escaped prisoner, even if it was from a southern prison. The senator stated that if she was responsible for the death of an officer, even a Confederate one, that might hold weight with the courts. He would look into it.

After the revelation that Philip was the father of a black bastard son, several businesses ceased to be associated with his firm, and social invitations were few and far between. It was one thing to support the end of slavery, but relationships between the races were frowned upon. Philip found it necessary to dismiss several employees and move to a smaller office. The overseas firm was doing well, and a new office had opened in Switzerland.

Unknown to Philip, his name had come up in Washington regarding an ambassadorship, perhaps to France or Belgium. His aid in securing the treaty with Uta during the war had not been forgotten.

He received a registered letter asking him to come to Washington for a meeting with President Grant. At his meeting with the President, Philip learned that if confirmed by the Senate, he would be offered the ambassadorship to France. He had thanked the president for considering him for such a prestigious position but felt he must discuss it with Bridget.

While in Washington, he also inquired about the progress in making a case against Annabelle. His friend had turned it over to the military courts. They had contacted Nathan's senior commander, but there was no additional information. Philip would be notified if any further action was taken.

After arriving home, he wasted no time sharing the news of his pending appointment with his wife. How would Bridget feel about leaving her home in America and moving halfway around the world? The children would benefit from learning a new language, and there was a world-renowned music school for Catherine. Thanks to Annabelle's public revelations, they had become pariahs in Boston. Why not begin again in a new place?

Bridget was stunned by his news. Leave their home? Move to Europe where they knew no one? What about Martha Montgomery? The children looked upon her as their grandmother. How could they leave her?

Philip asked her to think about it. He wasn't sure there was a future for them here. The children had been popular and had many friends in school, but now they were shunned. They couldn't understand why the other children had taken to calling them nasty names, and Catherine often came home crying. Did Bridget think any of this would change?

Philip had made an excellent point. The children were unhappy, and the small group of friends she had made had disappeared. Women wouldn't speak to her on the street if they met, and some would cross to the other side to avoid her.

Mrs. Montgomery agreed with Philip. There was little chance of things getting better. Bridget had left Ireland to make a new life for herself. She had done so alone, and with each new move, she had been alone. This time, Philip and the children would be there to share the adventure.

Philip returned to Washington with his family, and after being confirmed by the Senate, he accepted the Ambassadorship. Bridget had been presented to President Grant and soon became the sweetheart of the in-crowd.

Bridget was in great demand as a guest when she returned to Boston to pack up the house. She had no illusions as to why. All those who had shunned her earlier bent over backward to be her friends. Bridget politely declined their invitations. They wouldn't have given her the time of day if she hadn't been an ambassador's wife.

Chapter 66

Beginning Once Again

While in Washington, Philip spoke with President Grant about Annabelle. Grant had been in charge of the Union Army during the war. Philip relayed everything that had taken place, including how Annabelle had caused his brother to be charged with aiding the enemy and hung as a deserter. Having escaped punishment, she was now living in Boston.

Grant couldn't stomach the thought of someone switching loyalties every time the wind changed, and the fact that Annabelle had been convicted by a court, even if it was a Confederate court, rankled. She had been the reason for Nathan's desertion and his hanging. Because Annabelle had been responsible for the death of a soldier, even a Union soldier, during wartime, she must be considered a murderer. An order for her arrest was drawn up and sent to the authorities in Boston. Philip hoped that Annabelle would finally receive the punishment she deserved. She must pay for all the harm she had caused.

Mrs. Montgomery had decided to leave the school in younger hands. She, too, was prepared to leave her home and sail into a new life with her adopted family. She couldn't bear the thought of being separated from these people who had become so important to her. "Grandma Memee," as the children called her, would travel with them. Bridget and the children were relieved. They had dreaded the thought of her remaining behind. An essential piece of their family would have been missing.

Philip had informed his solicitor of the pending legal actions concerning his sister-in-law. They were to send him any information they received from the courts about Annabelle. He was prepared to return to Boston to testify against her if necessary. The case seemed open and shut, but Annabelle was a cat with nine lives.

When the day finally came, Philip and Bridget stood on the deck, gazing at the shoreline slowly fading away. Soon, it would be out of sight. The children were inspecting their quarters, excited to see the bunk beds and the ladder that led up to them. When they next reached land, there would be a train ride. All this was new and wonderful. They didn't share their parents' sadness at leaving the place where they had met and lived for so long.

Martha Montgomery joined them on deck. When the land had disappeared completely, they turned and walked to the front of the ship. It would be days before they reached France, but they were on their way. Philip put his arms around the two women. Once again, Bridget was starting over, but this time she wasn't alone.

About the Author

Julia is a cosmetologist and owns her own salon. As an actress, director, and costumer she works in local theaters. Julia belongs to a healing ministry and is ordained.

She was born in England and moved to Canada during WW2. She has lived in such diverse places as the Yukon, England, France, and Germany. Julia now lives in Texas with her life partner and a very bossy chihuahua.

Milton Keynes UK
Ingram Content Group UK Ltd.
UKHW020730130524
442628UK00001B/26

9 798224 339747